MEM-CO

MEM-CO

CALEB FEWIN

CONTENTS

A humming red skyline stretched across a dark blue sea of clouds. Calmly, the sun lowered toward the sandy shore. Palm trees softly swayed. A sweet Piña Colada rested quietly in its coconut cup, reflecting the straw hut and its dangling strands of light bulbs. Seagulls called out in the distance as a crab dragged itself across the wet sand. A woman in a small crimson bikini walked by holding a plate of cooked lobster and shrimp, ready to enjoy. She smiled lightly, reflecting the warm sunset as the sound of the waves hitting the shore softly swayed across the beach.

"How much?" Madox threw the mem-caster onto the counter.

He stood in an old, rundown gas station. Streaks of unknown black stains marked the rustic white floors. An orange bulb ticked softly in the back. Harsh fluorescent lights held the room in a lifeless glare. The open door to the bathroom revealed a mold-covered toilet, with water stains pooling on the blackened-orange tiles. A man in the back slumped drunkenly near the rear wall, holding a six-pack of beer worth more than the old gray shirt riddled with holes.

The cashier's gray shirt tightened over his belly. His jeans looked as though they hadn't been washed in months. Greasy hair circled his head, while his old, scruffy beard crept down his neck.

"You look at that one every day, and you never have enough for it. Stick to the level ones," he shot in a crooked tone.

"I don't care. I can't remember Anna," Madox objected. "How much?"

His tired dark brown eyes wore tear stains beneath them. His clean black shirt and pants stood out in the foul store. He wore straight black hair and a smooth, blemish-free face, other than the dried tear stains falling under his sagged eyelids. His nose was small and straight. His lips hung open as they pressed into his chest.

"Four hundred eighty bucks, final offer," the cashier snarled back.

"Four eighty!? You have to be kidding!" Madox shot back angrily.

"A level three memory for nine hours? That's a bargain, and you know it! Like I said, every day you come here and get the level one memories because that's all you can afford, you leech of a man!"

Madox's foot tapped wildly on the floor. *Every day? Do I really erase work every day? Should I keep doing this? Keep pouring out my mind like it's a disease that's going to kill me? Yes. Yes, I have to. I can't live with the guilt. I need something, anything, to get rid of the pain.*

"Fine, let me look at a level one." Madox realized he wouldn't have another option.

"Finally, here, look at this one," the cashier loaded a small cassette into the black box on the backside of the headset, handing it back to Madox.

A gray room sits silently as the bright white window spills a ray of light onto the empty wooden floor. The curtains flutter lightly in the wind as the image of a cool summer lake forces a sigh past ungrateful eyes. The feel of the wrinkled wooden handle lingers as the broom sweeps across the dirtied floor. Boss sits silently at the table, sipping her Buddy's Beer, glowing next to her. The lights on her phone flash on her empty face, scrolling along the wonderful colors of Mem-Book. Though there was no anger or sadness in the air, only a gentle breeze of work needing to be done before any fun could begin. The sound of the broom bristles scraping across the tiled floor as the work continued on for eternity.

"Fuck me! You expect me to take that shit?!" Madox threw the headset back on the counter.

"Well, it's that, or you drop four eighty on 'beach time fun,'" he read the label off the first cassette. "Or you can just leave me alone and get the hell out of my store, I ain't looking for trouble."

Anger boiled in Madox's stomach as the question of which memory would be worse swirled in his head.

"Fuck it, how much is it?" he gave in.

"Five bucks," the cashier's smile branded itself to Madox's chest like red-hot metal.

Madox handed over the money and stormed out of the building, gripping the cassette with the writing 'Sweeping' on the side. He opened the door to his small, black, rusty car with a check engine light held under Schrödinger's thumb for the past three years. Darkness filled the air, broken only by the single orange streetlight hovering over the pothole-filled parking lot. The bulb was so faint that even the puddles along the wet road couldn't reflect its pathetic light.

Sitting inside the car, Madox picked up the AMT sitting in the passenger seat. The device was small and white, with two straps crossing one another and a third running around the bottom, forming a hat-like shape meant to be worn on the head. A small white box sat at the back, with two hanging metal lights pointed directly into the eye sockets. Madox opened the small white box and placed the cassette into the slot, taking out a separate cassette with the writing 'Birthday Cleanup' on the side. He put on the AMT and grabbed the controller off the dashboard.

He set the time knob between '8 AM' and 'PRESENT', as he looked at the time displaying 6:15 on the radio clock. He closed his eyes and took a deep breath, reliving everything he couldn't bear to remember one last time.

Flick

The sound of light puffing in his eyes flew as boredom fell in his chest like a rock falling in a pond. All he could think about was how much he wanted to feel the cool, clear lake despite the work needing to be done. He took off the AMT, throwing it in the passenger seat.

Dust Pan —
Boring day
Get to work
No play
So empty
Let me go

"I could go for a Buddy's Beer at the lake," he said to himself with a deep sigh.

His mind quickly moved to the question of what he was doing. He looked around the car for any clues, barely noticing something on his left hand. 'Mem-Co 9AM-6PM' was written in black ink across his palm. He looked at the clock on the radio displaying the time 6:17.

"I just got off work, it's time to go home," he said to himself.

He took a withered sigh before putting the AMT back in the passenger seat. He quietly set the car in drive and began home, with nothing but the black wind to accompany him along the way. His mind circled around the gray, blurred room as the feeling of the wooden broom stuck to his fingertips. He could smell the dust through the static air and hear the sound of the Buddy's Beer flowing down his boss's lips. It was like hearing the whisper of a reality he never knew, hiding under a facade of nostalgia.

Over time, the feeling of boredom faded as a feeling of guilt grew in his stomach. Like a déjà vu of emotion rather than a memory, Madox was filled with unexplainable guilt. Even though the memory was gone, his body and brain could remember through muscle memory, like a shadow from the past wrapped around his neck.

"Ignorance is bliss," he whispered with a sigh, remembering his slogan-filled Mem-Co-provided childhood, allowing peace to enter his body. "Ignorance is bliss."

Gas Station —
Dark
Worn lights
Dried tears
Sorrow
Bliss?

Tall, overarching pine trees stood still in the yard, allowing the dull moon to pass briefly through their thin needles. The brown wooden fence surrounded the nicely kept lawn between the shoulder-pressed neighboring yards. The house was large yet empty, with a single light lit in the door window. Darkness hid the flowerbeds holding sunburnt mulch and underwatered flowers, as pockets of weeds flourished all about. A single bug-infested light sat on the front porch, turning the white walls orange as the light crept into the inky black forest.

Madox pulled into the driveway, lifting the garage door with his remote control. He slowly rolled his way in, closing the door behind him. The garage was mostly empty, with a small shelf in the corner holding scattered tools, and an antique push mower sitting beside it.

He opened the door and got out, slamming it shut behind him. He decided to leave the AMT in the passenger seat, as he wouldn't need it the rest of the night. He walked through the inside garage door, finding his wife, Kris, with a mem-caster strapped to her head. In one hand, she held her phone open to Mem-Book as its colorful lights flickered along the screen, while the other held an empty wine glass. She sat in the living room with her head lying back along the top of the couch. She was thin with long black hair, wearing a worn yellow dress covering her entire body. Her pale skin melted along her rounded body and wrinkled face.

Wine Glass —
A lazy day

Never awake
Only dreaming
Keep away
Don't let me remember

The room held a yellow-tinted light covering the pale, empty walls. A fireplace sat under the TV without a flame for over twenty years. The door to the kitchen was a shiny oak sitting over the dirty white carpeted floors. The hallway light leading to the bedroom was turned off, covering the faint breeze of the dusty air vent, letting out a constant white noise. Madox lightly closed the door, making just enough noise for her to notice.

"Oh, honey, you're home! You have to check out this new memory my friends have been telling me all about! It's a level three, and it has you sitting so cozy in a nice little cabin in the woods with nothing but you and a warm cup of hot chocolate," she said, waving her hand while the rest of her body stood still on the couch. "I just can't figure out what memory to replace it with. Would it be okay if I replaced our dinner on Tuesday with this one? It wasn't really that exciting, and I remember the waitress acting weird around us."

Like a fuse sizzling off right before hitting the dynamite, Madox's first feeling was anger as they didn't have enough money to afford level three memories. *How could she have bought that without consulting me?* Yet, his anger quickly faded as this was the normal routine. Even if he did confront her, there was no guarantee she would remember it the next day.

The fact that she wanted to replace their dinner on Tuesday didn't bother him nearly as much as the fact that he knew on Tuesday they didn't go to dinner together. It was just another night like this one, yet Madox couldn't remember what had happened Tuesday night. Like a blur on a window, each day was the same in and out, leaving nothing but a memory copied and pasted from 6:15 to 10:30 each night.

But why not use her childhood space? They give us an entire five years of blank memories to fill with whatever we want. Given how many memories she's replaced, she probably doesn't have any room left to fill. Another sigh fell from his exhaustion as he threw his nice black shirt and pants on the couch, leaving nothing but a pair of white boxers and a white shirt.

"Yeah, do whatever you want, I don't care," he told her, heading to the kitchen to make himself dinner.

Making dinner, Madox realized he didn't know what to make, or even what he liked. The difference between personal and corporate memories blurred to the point where he couldn't tell if the sweet, warm apple pie he had for his birthday last year was real or not. He couldn't make out the taste of an apple, as so many memories had different flavors and feelings surrounding them. The only taste he could remember was the taste of Buddy's Beer, humming so blissfully smooth in his mouth. He decided to make a bologna sandwich, more so because it was quicker and easier than because it was what he wanted.

He walked back out, Kris still sitting motionless on the couch. He sat next to her, switching the plate of sandwiches with the TV remote on the coffee table in front of them. He sat back, flipping through the TV, which he used more to dull out his surroundings than make him feel any better. He couldn't remember what kind of TV he enjoyed watching; all he knew was that it was something to make him stop thinking about the world, allowing him to temporarily void himself of his troubles.

Flickering Lights —
Numb
Consume
Feel good
Lose Consciousness
Alter present reality

The pendulum swung back and forth as they both sat silently on the couch together, yet in different worlds. Madox's mind was empty, filling itself with whatever colors and sounds fluttered on the screen, allowing a moment of rest.

Around ten, Madox looked at the black circular clock mounted just above the doorframe, realizing it was time to get ready for bed. He took a slow breath, knowing he wasted yet another forgotten night doing nothing but watch TV. *Maybe I can use that cabin memory if Kris doesn't use it to replace tonight... There's no way I'll get that memory...*

He began preparing for bed by taking a shower and brushing his teeth. Then, just before lying down, he checked on Kris one last time, who was in the same position as when he found her. She would stay up as late as she could every night to have room for all the memories she buys. She understood memories couldn't just be attached here and there, but to put a memory in one had to come out. So staying up later allowed her more space to put memories. She would even buy multiples of the same memory, like buying multiples of the same puzzle to reuse a piece she liked. Unfortunately for her and Madox's wallet, each cassette was a one-time use.

Madox found his way to bed alone, just like every other night. Thinking the same thoughts of fear and guilt, not knowing what he actually did for a living. *How bad could it be?* He tried to calm himself down. He lifted his left hand, looking at the ink marks staring him down like a duel at high noon. *If I need memories to cover up how bad work is every day, it must be terrible, right?* He couldn't help but flip over with the sounds of the voices in his head. Feelings of dread whispered in his ears like the phantom of memories yearning to be unearthed.

He looked up at the poster of Veltik standing proudly across a torn battlefield. 'Fight for Truth! Fight for Mem-Co!' Plastered itself at the bottom of the poster, as Veltik's bulky body held a gun in its arms and a cigarette in its mouth. Madox could feel Veltik's eyes staring into him, as though warning him not to give in to his pain and not to remember everything that made him upset.

"Ignorance is bliss," he spoke to himself before slowly falling asleep.

Dr. Veltik —
Big man
The leader
Is he real?
Why can't I remember?
Why can't I erase?

The next morning, Madox woke up, still alone in bed. The sound of his alarm on his nightstand was practically shouting, 'Work! Work! Work!' tying a knot in his stomach. He lay flat on his back, trying to calm himself before having to get up. *What am I going into?* Questions riddled his head like a shadowed figure lurking through the dark woods.

He slowly got up and went, putting on his normal black shirt and pants, along with brushing his teeth. He made sure to put on his long black necktie, using the mirror to help him get the knot just right. Walking into the living room, he noticed Kris still on the couch. She was asleep with the mem-caster still strapped to her head. Her right arm was stretched along the seats, holding her fallen wine glass with a drop of wine still dangling on its side.

Necktie —
A man going to work
A sign of respect
Treat me right
Don't ask about life
I just want to live

Madox walked like the wind into the kitchen, making sure not to wake her up. He began making breakfast, which was much easier than dinner because all they had were frozen waffles tucked deep into the freezer. While he was cooking, he heard the faint sound of footsteps beside him.

"Hey baby..." Kris said, wrapping her arms around Madox and putting herself up on him. She pulled her leg up, brushing her crotch against his hip as her lips grazed his neck.

"Last night was amazing, baby..." she said with a sinful smile.

Madox grit his teeth, knowing the most interesting thing that happened last night was the battle between the air conditioner and the single white sock dangling off his dresser. However, this was definitely not the first time Kris had done this, to the point where Madox knew exactly what to do in the situation.

"Oh yeah, it was..." he said, like reading the script off a teleprompter. "I have to go to work now, but just wait until tonight."

She grinned wildly, wrapping her hands around his head while Madox wrapped his hands around her waist, knowing the chances of her remembering this conversation by tonight were one in a thousand. She gave him a peck on the cheek and let him go.

"Alright, well, you get to work, and I'll see you tonight," she grinned happily, walking back over to the couch.

Madox looked to the floor, wiping his eyes as though he were cleansing his brain from the thought of her. He grabbed his waffles as they popped out of the toaster and headed to the door.

"See you tonight, baby!" Kris yelled as he shut the door to the garage.

With another long sigh, he got inside the car, checking his hand still holding the grimy black letters engraved like stone. *Why don't I remember anything about work? What can be so bad that I have to erase everything I do every day?* The knot in his stomach continued to churn. He opened the garage door and pulled out, starting his drive to Mem-Co.

CHAPTER 2

After a short drive through the tall pine woods and past the old rustic gas station he avoided as much as possible, Madox arrived at Mem-Co. The building was huge, about five stories tall, and stretched like a forest into the deep woods. Its white brick walls and large black letters on the front spelling 'Memory Corporation' greeted him like metal bars overlooked by a spotlight.

He pulled into the three-hundred-vehicle parking lot, lucky to find a spot near the back, forcing him into a five-minute walk to the glass revolving door entrance. His heart pounded as his stomach tightened, pressing into his chest. *What am I walking into? What could possibly be so horrible about this place?* Questions stuck like weights holding him down with each step.

"Good morning, Mr. Rightly! Mr. Dayfell is waiting for you in the lab department, just head down this hall and to the left!" the door greeter said, pointing down the hall with a smile on her face, sending a shot of relief through Madox's body.

"Thanks," he said with a light nod.

"Of course! Have a great day!" she said just as cheerfully.

Heading down the unknown hall, Madox's body knew exactly where to go. He felt like a mouse in a maze, knowing the exact route to take to find the cheese, despite having no memory of ever being in the maze.

The walls were a pale blue, as though the white paint was holding onto the memory of once holding color. Signs were posted everywhere, displaying slogans Madox had seen a hundred times.

Don't argue, just remember!
Don't choose sadness, choose Mem-Co!
Learn the fun and fast way with Mem-Co!
Mem-Co, where your dreams come true!
Peace! That's what we're all about!
Ignorance is bliss!
Keep your Reality Relative!
Memories are Reality!

Madox could feel his chest relax as the soft phrases from his child-hood began to calm him down. *Don't argue, just remember. Maybe I should get a memory so I don't have to remember Kris for a while.*

Eventually, he reached the lab department, a large open room the size of a three-story building. Hundreds of people were seated at desks and tables, wearing black suits and white lab coats. Their fingers typed away on keyboards like a chattering symphony of engines fueled by coffee and corporately funded memories, soon to replace their work. Glass rooms held clipboards and experiments, with subjects wearing mem-casters and AMTs. Men in black padded suits stood at the doorways holding police batons and tasers on their waist belts.

"Madox, you're finally here!" a man shouted, appearing from behind a desk. He was tall and somewhat built, wearing a white lab coat and black pants. He had straight brown hair and happy blue eyes, holding a smile too genuine to be real.

"I'll show you where you need to go, and here take this," he said, leading Madox through the lab, and handing him a cassette with 'For Madox' printed on the side. The man walked briskly through the quiet yet relentless room, leaving Madox struggling to keep up. They reached an isolated set of black doors with two bodyguards stationed at each side.

"Identification," one of the men said robotically.

"Don't worry, I have yours," the man said, pulling out two ID cards.

He handed them to the guard, who scanned them on the wall next to the door, letting out a green flick for each card. The guard handed them back and opened the door to let them through, not saying a word.

"Thanks!" the man said, walking through the door.

Madox followed close behind him, having no idea what was happening. *Is this Mr. Dayfell that the receptionist mentioned? Does he do this every day? Where am I going that needs so much security?* The knot in his stomach grew to where he thought he could hear it groaning.

They reached a narrow hallway holding nothing but a second set of doors at the end, this one far more guarded than the first. Twenty men stood on each side of the hall, holding black machine guns along with their utility belts. Ten cameras surrounded every inch of the hallway, along with a set of panels next to the doors looking more like a metal vault than a working environment.

"Oh, I never remember to introduce myself! My name is Selleck Dayfell, and don't worry about all this; they just need to make sure nobody sees what's inside. Just company secrets we don't want out, you understand," Selleck said, trying to reassure Madox yet making him more on edge than before.

"You know, there are only about thirty people on the planet that know what's behind these doors, and you are one of them. So take pride in that! I'll go in and help you get started, but the cassette I gave you should explain most everything once you see what's going on."

He gave the IDs to the man standing next to the side panels, who checked them once again. After handing back the IDs, a set of men came from the line and began patting them down. Madox's brain and stomach boiled in anticipation of what could be behind the doors, and how he could have any relevance to whatever it was.

Once the men were done with their inspection, the man next to the panel called out, "Ready, front! Move out!" The command sent every man out the original doors, leaving only Madox and Selleck.

"Like I said, there are very few people who know what's in these doors. Not even the guards are allowed to see what's inside," Selleck said joyfully.

Selleck went to the panel and clicked a button, sending sounds of air and turning gears all around the massive metal door. Madox's chest was like a drum as his stomach did its best to keep his vomit from his anxiety inside. The door swung open, revealing the horror Madox feared yet couldn't have imagined.

A massive room, long and wide enough that Madox couldn't see the end, filled with children around the ages of thirteen to eighteen, strapped to chairs. They had tubes of clear and yellow liquids shooting out of them, along with a black fused mem-caster-AMT device strapped to their heads, covering from their eyes upward. They sat with loose necks in thick black chairs, all wearing the same dull gray outfit covering their entire body.

Lifeless Bodies —
Who can help them?
What is Mem-Co?
Why do we hide?
Please let me die
Why is knowledge so painful?

Madox fell to his knees as tears ran down his face, realizing why he needed to take out the memory of this place every single day. *What is this? Why are they doing this? How are they doing this? It doesn't make sense!* His mind was riddled with conflict and questions.

"I bet you're wondering what all this is. The cassette I gave you should explain most everything," Selleck said, handing him an AMT. "It's only a ten-minute memory; you usually use the drive here to replace it with."

Madox took the AMT with shaky hands, taking out the cassette labeled 'For Madox' and replacing it with the new one. He set the time to replace the memory of his drive and placed it on his head.

Flick

A completely white room with the shadow of a man sitting in a chair.

"Hi Madox! I bet you're wondering what's going on here, and that's what I'm here to tell you!" It began. "As you already know, when children are first born, they are taken by Mem-Co. This is because the early stages of life are a crucial aspect of who people become as adults. So at Mem-Co, we allow every child the exact same childhood, preventing unwanted attributes of things like divorce, alcoholism, and beliefs of their parents and culture from affecting their lives. We even allocate a five-year period of silence for the children to be able to put whatever memories they want when they are older. This then allows everyone to grow up with similar beliefs and attributes, preventing unwanted hatred and beliefs between people, and cultivating peaceful living. We even replace the parents' memories of having children with level four or five memories, allowing parents freedom to have no kids, along with a memory of their choosing to better their lives. This then effectively allows people the opportunity to do whatever they want in life, no matter how abstract or abnormal from their ordinary lives. However, what most people don't know is what exactly the children do while they are here with us at Mem-Co. For the first twelve years of life, the children are exposed to normal childhood activities and social constructs, with constant supervision, of course. At this time, we also heavily enforce basic reading, writing, and math until it becomes muscle memory, unable to be erased by overwriting memories. Then, between the ages of thirteen and eighteen, when their brains are more developed, we hook them to the Memory-Construct Network, or MCN, for short. You see, making memories is not as easy as making a movie and sending it into your brain. Making memories requires a dimension of rendering that computers cannot capture. What dimension is that? Feelings! Memories have an ele-

ment of feeling, whether it be happiness, anger, fear, or whatever else it may be. So then the question came about, how do we put feeling into a memory? That's where the MCN comes in. You see, the MCN connects the brains of the children and uses it to render the feelings computers are unable to compute. Now you may be thinking to yourself, how this may seem unethical, or not right. However, we here at Mem-Co put a strong emphasis on peace and harmony. As such, we believe allowing children to have the memories of a good childhood and allowing everyone else on the globe the ability to use Mem-Co products is the best solution to world peace. And after the children turn nineteen, we give them better memories, so it's like they were never here in the first place. Remember, ignorance is bliss! But as you may be wondering, what is your purpose here at Mem-Co? Well, your job is simple: keep the children here on the MCN happy and healthy. You monitor their food levels, brain activity, and any other abnormalities to allow these children a happy adulthood, and provide the computing power needed to supply the world with instant happiness. Thank you for all that you do, Madox!"

The memory explained, then went into detail about the specifics of his job and all Madox had to do on a normal basis.

"How? What? This is insane!" Madox looked at Selleck as though he had just murdered someone in front of him.

"Insane? This is just business. And I mean, nobody's getting hurt because of it, right? The children will have their memories replaced with something much better when they are older. Before us, there would be kids starving in Africa and watching their parents beat one another. Now we all get the same childhood, no matter where you're born," Selleck rebutted.

"What about the parents? What about being a mom or dad?" Madox shot.

"What about them? They have a kid, then we give them a good memory after that. If they want a memory of a nine-month cruise on the Atlantic, then we give it to them. If they want non-stop sex with famous porn stars and actresses, let them have it. And if all they want is to be a mom or dad, we'll just give them the memory of having a wonderful child who grew up to be successful and make them proud. We're only helping the world here, Madox," Selleck said, as though he'd had to explain this a million times.

"Well, what if I leave? What if I go tell the world what you're doing to these kids, what Mem-Co has done to them?" Madox's disgust turned to anger.

"Then what? You think they'll believe you? They can't even distinguish their own lives from the corporate-filled reality Mem-Co gives them, so what makes you think they'll take anything you say seriously? Even if they did believe you, they'd probably just feel bad and overwrite that memory anyway, so what's the point?"

It felt as though Selleck put the barrel of a shotgun to Madox's heart and pulled the trigger. He could feel himself shake as the knot in his stomach boiled with rage, disgust, and confusion. *How can this be real? I want to get this memory out of my head as soon as I can.*

"Well, you'd better get to work, though. You don't want those children dying 'cause you didn't do your job," Selleck said, walking back through the door.

Madox sat on his knees for a while, taking in what had just been said to him. The reality of what he does and what the world is. But still, like every other day, he pulled himself up with tears rolling down his face and got to work.

The chiming of distant machinery rang like a knife spinning in Madox's chest. He held a clipboard, walking down the endless rows of mindless children, checking the small boxes as he worked on his daily maintenance routine. He had plenty to do while he worked, like checking the food levels of the tube-fed children and monitoring bowel and bladder levels to make sure everything was functioning properly. Even brain activity had to be monitored to make sure each child was not having their brain overclocked, causing possible brain damage and death.

The knot in Madox's stomach was like a black hole, sucking in his feelings of happiness and joy. His mind raced over everything he was doing and what he had learned. These poor children, he thought, looking over the ocean of innocent souls bound to their lifeless chairs like they were nothing more than the thousands of tiny transistors in a computer CPU. Luckily, the focus of his tasks was able to somewhat block out the thoughts of his own moral dilemmas. Still, every time he looked at the face of a child, the knot grew tighter. Madox's mind couldn't help but start itching to get out and replace his memory. Like a drug addict waiting for his next shot, allowing the blissful release of pain from this awful world.

As he was making his way down, he found an error with one of the children. A small girl, no older than fifteen, with bright blond hair and a tiny white face. Her eyes were rolled to the back of her head as drool spilled out of her mouth, like many of the other children trapped here. He could see the flashing of tiny white lights on the back of her head under her headset, showing her brain was in working condition and being used to generate memories.

However, Madox noticed blood spilling out of her ear. As such, he unhooked her from the machine and carried her unconscious body to the nursing quarters. He made his way into a blank metallic room with nothing but a dark blue table to put her on. He softly laid her down and ran into the next-door room, which held hundreds of colorful flashing buttons and screens. A window into the girl's room sat in the middle of the wall. Madox sat down and did a quick scan of her.

Number: 44934402
Name: Anna
Brain Activity: Positive
Age: 15
Additional Information:
Madox Entries: 28

Twenty-eight entries?! Why would there possibly be twenty-eight en-tries for this single girl that I've written? Something must be wrong. He clicked on the entries and began reading the last one.

Hey Madox, it's you from yesterday, most likely. So she's been having some kind of issue for about a month now, and she's still getting worse. Ap-parently, we already tried taking her to the hospital, but they won't let any of the kids out of here to get checked by a doctor because of how confidential this place is. Selleck said, "If she dies, she dies. It happens all the time. But who's going to know? Not their parents, not you. There's nothing you can do, Madox." And honestly, there is nothing we can do. We've tried every-thing. Just put her back. And fuck this place.

Madox ran to the nearby trash can in the corner and threw up as his stomach throbbed to the point he couldn't handle the pain. Tears rolled down his face as thoughts shot through his head. *I just have to let this lit-tle girl die? And there's nothing I can do about it?* His face turned pale as sweat dripped down his forehead, his shaky arms holding him above the trash can. *I need to get this memory out of my head. I need to rid myself of the memory of this place. I need it so badly.*

After a while, he calmed himself down enough to put the girl back where she was, knowing there was nothing he could do to help her. He continued his normal work, still thinking about Anna. As he was think-ing of her, he realized something. *How can I know for sure any of these kids isn't mine? If they replace the memories of the parents, then, as far as I know, I could be a father. Anna could be my daughter.* Vomit rolled up his throat as his thoughts overtook him.

Hours later, Madox finally clocked off work, his hands shaky and face pale as he made his way back through the heavily guarded facility. He walked through the room filled with chattering keyboards and down the hall of endless slogans. The sign, displayed in bright white and yel-low colors, 'Ignorance is bliss' spoke heavily to him. *I need to rid my memory of Anna.*

"Have a good evening, Madox! See you tomorrow," the lady at the front desk said, like a knife to his chest.

He hurried to his car and began driving away, looking for the nearest spot to buy a memory. Then he saw it, like an oasis in a desert, the rustic gas station he always passed by. He swerved into the parking lot and ran inside.

CHAPTER 3

The walls shouted like an ice-filled blender as the hundreds of people stood talking to one another. The room was lit with circular lights sticking into the black tiled roof. The large black screen covered the entire back wall, hovering ominously over the crowd of red velvet chairs stretched in rows up and down the auditorium.

Madox and Kris sat in the back left corner, as Kris talked Madox's ear off about the last time she traveled to Japan. Blocking Kris out, Madox looked around the room, seeing smiles strapped to the people greeting one another. *Just another community meeting.*

"Hi'ya Madox!" A familiar voice scratched Madox's ears.

He looked over to find his neighbors, Ralph and Julia Limon. They both wore thick black glasses with matching green outfits. Ralph had freckles with dark brown hair, while Julia had deathly white skin and straight dirty-blond hair.

"Hi Ralph!" Kris sparked, excited to see them.

"So how's it going? Been a while since we've caught up," Ralph asked with his perfect set of teeth shining through his welcoming smile.

"Oh, it's been great! I was just telling Madox about my trip to Japan on Friday, it was amazing! I wish I had brought pictures with me to show you!" Kris shouted off excitedly.

"Oh, that's just wonderful!" Julia stepped in softly. "I know Ralph here just got back from his trip to Colorado, show them the thing!" She tapped on his shoulder wildly.

"Oh, honey," Ralph smiled, pulling out a small mountain dangling upside down from his keychain. "A souvenir I bought at a gift store after fishing on the most beautiful lake I have ever seen. The clear water, scenic mountains rising past the beautiful forest of pine trees, and just the feeling of nature. It was wonderful."

"That sounds amazing!" Kris said, captured by Ralph's story.

Just as Kris was about to continue, the lights dimmed, and the crowd began to move to their seats.

"Ope we better get to our seats, it was great catching up!" Ralph said kindly, as he and Julia waved away.

Another minute passed before everyone sat down, leaving the room completely silent. A loud flash came from the back wall as the screen lit up in bright flashing colors. The title of the movie flashed in large black text, 'Star Battle: Return of the Wonder Girl' as the movie began to play. Madox watched the lights flash across the crowd of smiling faces as the images appeared on the screen.

Looking over the crowd, he noticed a woman with red hair sitting a few rows down. He glanced at her as her beautiful face flashed on the screen. Turning his eyes to Kris, he sighed as her mundane beauty revealed itself. He turned back to the woman with red hair, and to his surprise, saw that her head was turned back, looking at him. She quickly flipped her head back to the screen, sending Madox into shock. *Who is that woman?* He thought to himself for a while, until his mind turned off to the flashes of the screen.

Around an hour and a half passed, and the movie was over, greeted with a grand applause booming from the crowd. Personally, Madox thought the film was a seven out of ten. The story was great, but unfortunately, the actors in most of the sex scenes weren't his type.

The lights turned back on as a group of people in black clothing walked along the edges of the rows, passing buckets filled with cassettes and AMTs. Reaching Madox, he took out a cassette and AMT and put it on his head, setting the time from an hour and a half ago to the present. He looked over to see that Kris had already put the AMT on her head.

Flick

"I promise," she said without hesitation after a light flash shot from her eyes.

Madox looked straight at the blank screen before taking a deep sigh.

Flick

The wind screamed wildly, piercing like icicles through the rough, cool air. Hands gripped the jacket, unable to provide protection from the deadly scream. Looking forward, a large crooked building of cracked red bricks stood under the gloomy gray sky. Broken glass and rusty bars lay open to the looming air.

Body shaking as the door swung open to go inside. The air was stale as the torn walls of gray stretched along the ill-lit hallway. People smelling of urine and dirt, dressed in ragged clothing and unwashed faces, sat along the floors, covered in warm blankets and smiles as their spoons dipped into the steaming bowls of inviting stew.

White light poured out of the window, sitting atop the kitchen connected to the hallway. A man dressed in a faint brown and red plaid sweater stood behind the kitchen counter, scooping soup into bowls as a line of people stood joyfully, anticipating their food. The man had a kind smile with a handsome face and muscles popping lightly out of his sweater.

"You are so amazing, thank you so much for all you have done for us," a woman said as tears dripped from her eyes after being handed her bowl by the man.

"Of course, I love having the opportunity to serve our community and help those in need," he said in a deep, friendly voice, as the woman walked away. "Oh, it's you! So glad you could join me. My name is Dr. Veltik. Would you like some soup and a nice warm blanket?" The man asked as the line seemed to have disappeared.

Veltik handed over a warm, deliciously smelling bowl of soup as though he wrapped the warmth of the sun into a ball. The soup tasted of stars as the heat filled the coolness of the galaxy. The feeling of safety and comfort radiated through the air. Veltik sat down, looking at all the people smil-

ing so joyfully, as though a father watching his children. His smile beamed warmer than even the soup, as his face looked over.

"Yes, I love going to homeless shelters and helping all the wonderful people living there. You can learn so much from their incredible stories and warming tales. It's just so awful what happened to all these wonderful people," he said in a low tone.

"What happened to them?"

"Oh, don't you know? This is what happens to people who choose to remember. They can't let go of a job, a person, or so many other things, and it slowly drives them down a dark path in life. It's so sad to see these beautiful faces driven here due to their own knowledge. Do you see her?" His hand pointed at the woman, still teary-eyed over the soup she was given. "Her name is Linda Pertrude. She was actually once the CEO of a multi-million dollar company. Unfortunately, one day, her husband was in an accident, killing him instantly. She was devastated, but for some reason she chose to remember him. She chose to live in the grief and pain of her husband's death, crying herself to sleep every night, thinking about him. Her pain overtook her, and she eventually stopped going to work, causing her to get fired and eventually lose everything she had built. All because she chose to live in pain, instead of bliss.

Luckily, now she is here, and we have given her better memories to erase her husband's death. Every time I come here, I get to see the beautiful smile on her face. Promise me you won't be like these people, won't be like her. If something is making you unhappy, always remember something else. It would make me so happy to see that you are happy too. Remember, ignorance is bliss. Promise me you will remember bliss."

"I promise," Madox spoke softly as tears filled his eyes.

Part Two

Later that day, Madox found himself in Memory Hall, dragged along by Kris because she wanted a conjoined memory of them solving a detective's case together. The building was a two-hundred-meter square of metal walls and a twenty-meter-tall roof holding dangling white LED panels. Hundreds of people stood in seven long lines stretched from the entry doors to the worker desks placed on the opposite end. The two were about halfway through the third line from the left, having waited over half an hour so far.

The room was loud, as hundreds of people talked with one another. The ones that weren't talking scrolled their phones, watching the endless colors and noises of Mem-Book. Kris wasn't any different, almost shouting just for Madox to hear her.

"Aren't you so excited!" She gripped Madox's arm and leaned in delighted. "We get to be detectives! I've heard this one is the best! I get to be the lead detective, though, right?"

"Sure," Madox said in an empty tone, halfheartedly listening to her while eavesdropping on the conversations around him.

"Well fuck you, Jim!" shouted a woman just up the line.

"Well fuck you too, Sharon!" a man shouted back in an equal tone.

Must be here to lose their memories of one another.

"-then the woman pulls out a gun! I'm not sure how we are going to get out of that situation, but I bet I do a kick-flip and-"

"Do you want to get a Buddy's Beer after this? After skydiving yesterday, I've just been craving Buddy's Beer so much, 'Have a buddy! Have a beer!

Mem-Co advertisement.

"-What do you think will be your favorite part? Mine will be the final reveal at the end, I'm just so excited to find out who did it-"

"This is going to be such an amazing honeymoon, a trip to Paris! We saved up for weeks to pay for this trip. I can't wait to remember it. Keep reality relative!"

How long have they been married? How long did it take them to save up for the memory of their honeymoon?

"-kill a guy? I hope not. I don't want the blood of a person on-"

"It's okay, I'm here for you. They'll replace your memories soon, and you'll feel so much better. Just try not to think of your dog anymore, okay. Remember, ignorance is bliss."

Dog died. Too bad.

"-It will hurt? I'll tell them I *cannot* do pain or blood or anything like that. Even thinking about it gives-"

"Well, I've always wanted to be a famous writer! I wonder what books I would have written. I think I want to be a comedy writer. That would be fun. I just love Mem-Co! Where dreams come true!"

Becoming a writer? He must be rich.

"Are you even listening?!" Kris shouted as Madox broke from his trance. "The lady asked for your name!"

Madox realized he was somehow standing at the front of the line. A cute curly-haired woman sat behind a glass divider, smiling at him warmly. Behind her stood a memory policeman, ominously watching in his black attire.

"Oh, Madox, Madox Rightly..."

"Perfect, and you said you will be the lead detective while Madox will be the side detective, correct?" she asked as her fingers chattered away on the computer in front of her.

"Yes, and could you make sure I don't have to kill anyone or get hurt? I really hate pain," Kris responded as a chill ran down her spine.

"Will do! Of course, we couldn't give memories that cause you or anyone else pain anyway," she smiled with a laugh.

"Oh, that's a relief!" Kris continued to hold onto Madox's arm, squeezing him tight.

"This is a twenty-four-hour memory, so what memories were you wanting to replace them with?"

"All of last Thursday would be great!" Kris chirped.

"Sounds great! That's all I need! If you'll just head around back, we have a few memory police ready and waiting to get you the memories you deserve! Thank you for choosing Mem-Co!" the lady announced, handing a piece of paper to the man in black clothing behind her.

The two walked around to the left side of the desks, through a set of double doors guarded by two memory police. Inside, there was a set of seven rooms, one of which was open, with a guard standing in the doorway.

"Mr. and Mrs. Rightly?" The man asked, holding up the piece of paper that the desk lady had made.

"Yes, that's us!" Kris shouted excitedly.

"Come in here," the man waved them in.

The two walked into a small, dimly lit room with two beds on either side. The man walked in behind them, shutting the metal door. He held two cassettes, an AMT, and a memory locator.

"Both of you, please sit on opposite beds," the man said, and the two did as they were told.

The man placed the memory locator on the back of Kris's head, displaying all her memories as he looked to find the exact time to place the memories. Soon, after the man was done, he walked over and did the same for Madox. The memory locator was a thick but short black stick with a screen on one end, next to the tip, to view the memories. After checking Madox's memories, the man placed the memory locator in his belt. He then gave the AMT to Kris, who immediately put it on.

"You will both need to lie down while I give you your memories," the man said, sending both Kris and Madox to lie on their backs.

The man walked over and lifted Kris's head up to place the cassette in the AMT. Reaching into his pocket, Kris couldn't help but smile from ear to ear.

Flick

Kris's smile suddenly died into an unconscious sleep. The man quickly removed the AMT and replaced the cassette. Madox could feel his foot begin to swing in the open air, unable to tap the ground. The man walked over and lifted Madox's head, placing it on his head. He reached back into his pocket.

Flick

Slowly, Madox's eyes opened as a large yawn broke from his face. His head flung around until finding the clock shouting in his ear that it was time for work. Beginning to crawl out of bed, he noticed Kris was just now waking up along with him.

"Hey there, partner? Where do you think you're going?" she asked seductively. "I have another case to solve back in bed..."

She smiled widely as Madox couldn't help but sigh. It had been over a week since they solved the case, yet she continued to call him partner. He only allowed it while they were investigating, but she still hadn't stopped.

"Reality is relative," Madox let out another sigh before giving in to Kris.

CHAPTER 4

One evening, Madox found himself in his usual diner talking with his friend Denis. He was a tall, skinny man with blond hair and scattered light freckles across his average white face. Denis was Madox's best friend, and the only real escape he had from the endless bleeding of days into one another. They drank their usual Buddy's Beer, as the sign on the wall flickered 'Have a buddy! Have a Beer!'

The room was well-lit. Soft, radiant lights hovered over the endless crowd of people. They talked joyfully, scrolling their phones in their booths. Waitresses walked around smiling gladly in their tight, skimpy red outfits, with 'A Drink to Remember!' strapped in white letters on the top right of their shirts. The bartender stood silently smiling behind the counter, cleaning glasses while listening to the upbeat music playing on the jukebox just outside the bathrooms. The walls were covered with black and red tiles as the smell of salt and grease flooded the air.

"Yeah, she just keeps talking about that dang trip to Indonesia and how much fun it was. How does she not realize how stupid and fake everything she says sounds? No, you've never climbed a mountain or seen these wonderful views of places. I just wish she would realize how pointless those things are," Denis ranted loudly about his wife as Madox nodded his head in agreement, staring at his drink.

"Yeah, I get how you feel. Just make sure you keep your voice down, alright," Madox told him softly.

"No, you're right, sorry. She just infuriates me sometimes," he responded, taking another swig of his beer.

Beer Bottle —
Angry
Sad
Please help
A lonely day
Don't let reality be real

"Jeremy! I love you!" shouted a teary-eyed woman, and she burst through the door. "Please come back to me! I miss you! I promise I can change!"

Everyone looked around, unsure who she was referring to.

"This is gonna get ugly..." Denis spoke, looking away from the woman.

She ran up to a man in a booth, seeming to have no idea who she was, then grabbed his hand without his permission.

"I don't know you!" he shouted, pulling her away.

"Yes, you do! I love you! Please!" she began to sob as Madox counted all the phones talking with the memory police.

"Get away from me! I don't remember you!" the man shouted, pulling out his phone to call them as well.

Suddenly, the door burst open once again, to find two beefy men in black padded clothing with 'MP' in white letters across the front. They looked around, quickly identifying the woman by her tear-stained eyes. The men rushed over as she pleaded for them to stop. Grabbing her arms, they pulled her away, slamming her head on a nearby table, right in the middle of a group of people having dinner.

One of the men pulled out a memory locator, placing it at the back of her head, as the other continued to hold her down. Tears streamed from her eyes as she shouted for help. There was nothing but a wave of silence as every eye watched what was happening. After a minute of looking into her memories, the man took off the ML and placed an AMT on her head. She began to scream as loud as she could until-
Flick

Her voice disappeared with her tears just as suddenly as the flash of light shot across her eyes. The man let her go, allowing her to stand back up, holding a beautiful smile on her face. The crowd cheered.

"Yeah, memory police! You rock!" a man shouted.

Even the woman cheered as they made their way back to the man at the booth. They quickly placed the AMT on him, as he was ready to have this memory removed, and with a light-

Flick

Everything was back to normal. The woman walked out smiling. People talked and scrolled as though nothing had happened.

"How many did you count?" Denis asked, still looking away from the crowd.

"Twelve, including the guy at the booth," Madox responded. "So anyway, how's work going?" Madox asked, taking in another drink of his beer.

"Not too bad, I got the new line of level five 'Island Resort' memories to start putting together. You're never going to believe it, but there's gonna be hot strippers in this one," Denis said sarcastically with a laugh.

"Heh, so when you gonna hook me up with one of those?" Madox said jokingly.

"So you wanna end up like my wife, too?" Denis shot back with a laugh. "And what about you, though? You still don't even know what you do for a living?"

Madox downed another drink, "Yep, no idea. And honestly, I don't want to know."

"But doesn't that make you just as bad as our wives? You really need a new job, man," he responded with brutal honesty.

"Don't try comparing me to them. They are hookers for memories, while I am just trying to sleep at night. Plus, I don't know the real reason I get rid of them, maybe it's just confidential, and they don't want me telling anyone." Madox responded, feeling the knot in his chest. "But whatever, how's it going with the whole doctor thing?" Madox tried switching the subject.

"Yeah, it's coming along. I'd say I'm about halfway through the cost I need to buy the medical knowledge I need to be a doctor. Another three years and I think I should be able to buy it."

"When you do get the money, you know what memories you're gonna replace, or where you want to work?"

"Well, the memory is eight months, so I was thinking I'd replace the eight months leading up to me buying it. Makes the most sense to me. And I'd definitely just go wherever is closest, no need to move far."

That was the answer Madox was expecting to hear. Most people work some boring job for the first five to ten years after childhood, then buy the knowledge of where they want to work and replace the memories of working at their old boring job.

"Yeah, just make sure to remember me," Madox said with a laugh.

"Remember what? You're ugly face or musty smell?" Denis said jokingly. "Of course I'll remember you. I need someone to rant to."

"Yeah, me too," Madox said, finishing off his beer. "Well, I'd better head home and make sure Kris didn't fry her brain on her AMT," he said, standing up.

"Well, see you later, call me whenever," Denis said, holding up his beer as Madox gave him a pat on the back and walked out the door.

Madox made his way back home, the knot in his stomach relentlessly eating away at his happiness. He found his mind racing over what he could possibly be doing for work. So, like usual, after he got home, he made himself food and watched TV, drowning out any possible thoughts of tomorrow.

A few more weeks flew by, as though each day was the swipe of a video on Mem-Book, doing nothing but blurring into the endless presence of time. Each night, he found Kris on the couch, hoping she would realize how pointless those memories were to her. Yet, nothing changed. It was as though the person he came home to was different, having to readjust to the stranger he lived with each and every night. But as long as he could block out the reality of the present with TV, he was just fine.

One evening Madox was watching his usual Thursday night football. The blue and white Good Guys up against the red and black Bad Guys, just like every game. The Good Guys wore a nice pink heart on their helmets and jerseys, while the Bad Guys were marked with an angry skull. Madox didn't know a soul rooting for the Bad Guys, as the entire stadium of blue cheered, 'Go Good Guys! Go Good Guys!' in unison. Madox even heard the players on the Bad Guys team had to wear masks to keep the players safe outside the stadium.

The score was twenty-six to twenty-seven, with the Bad Guys in the lead. The stadium booed and hissed as there was only a minute left in the last quarter, with the Bad Guys in possession of the ball. Tears of sadness and anger flew through the fans with the question, 'How can the Good Guys win?' eating at their brains. Yet for some reason, Madox wasn't scared of losing. He couldn't tell if it was from the fact their all-star player, Max Thump, was set front and center of the screen, waving confidently like he had everything under control, or the three hundred plus consecutive wins they've had for who knows how many years.

Fourth down came, and this was the Good Guys chance to win the ball back. Twenty-five seconds shot like a bomb about to blow up the stadium. Even though Madox knew they would win, he couldn't help but sit on the edge of the couch, staring as though he himself would be able to summon their victory.

Ding-Dong!

The doorbell rang just before the play.

"Who's that?" Kris asked, pulling up her AMT for the first time in what seemed to be three days.

"I don't know," Madox responded, focused on the game.

"Well, go check it out!" Kris waved him on.

The bell rang three more times before Madox sighed, walking to the door. *Who could this be? We never get guests other than Denis and his wife on special occasions.* Madox's mind raced with the question of who could possibly be at the door. He walked over and slowly opened it.

"Hi!" shot from a cheerful girl holding a billboard smile. She was skinny with a colorful yellow dress decorated with white flowers, and her face was smooth and warm. The way she looked at Madox was like a radiating glow of happiness and joy that he couldn't understand.

"My name is Natalie, but most people just call me Nat. Anyway, I'm here just going house to house inviting people to my church on Sunday!" she said cheerfully.

"Church?" Madox mumbled like it was a foreign word to him.

"Yes! We are the First Church of Love, just past the grocery store on Steward Street, and we would love it if you came and joined us Sunday!" she said just as cheerfully.

Madox was speechless for a moment, caught off guard by the mention of church.

"Uh, no, thank you, we're not interested," he managed to cough up a smile.

"No problem!" she said with joy still radiating from her body. "But remember to love everyone!" She finished and began walking off as Madox closed the door.

"Who was it?" Kris said, still holding the AMT off her head.

"Some girl asked if we wanted to go to church with her on Sunday," he responded, sitting back on the couch.

"Oh–did she say 'love everyone'?" she asked, almost jumping out of her seat.

"Yeah, how did you-"

"Yes, I've heard of them! Christians! Apparently, they have amazing memories and just give them out for free on Sundays. We should definitely go check them out," she said with the first smile on her face Madox had seen in weeks.

"Alright, I don't care," he said, turning the game back on, revealing the Good Guys' miraculous win. Kris did a happy little clap of excitement before going straight back into the AMT as though nothing had happened.

A few hours slipped away, sitting on the couch as the flashing lights and sounds of the TV entered Madox's brain. He tried to get the image of the girl out of his head, yet still, she sat in the back of his mind, holding thoughts and questions he would rather block out. *Christianity? Love everyone? That sounds like a load of crap.*

Madox had only one encounter with Christianity before, when he went to church with a girl he liked to try and get her to like him. He could remember the smell of the still oak air along with the color of her dark black hair. They sat in the third-to-last row, which was a long wooden bench holding three others on the other side. The walls were made of mismatched shades of gray bricks, as the lighting from the colorful stained glass windows allowed the sun to easily pierce through. He could remember the smell of her perfume as they sat and listened to the minister preach.

"Love everyone!" he shouted as the small crowd cheered him on.

"Amen!" shouted a woman behind us.

"Love everyone!" Madox's date, whose name he couldn't remember, shouted.

He could hardly even remember her face, come to think of it. They only went out on that one date, which he doesn't even know if he would consider a date. Still, there was a feeling in that memory he couldn't get out of his head. Happiness. A feeling he seemed to have a hard time finding in his mundane routine.

Maybe going to church would be a good idea. Maybe I might like it? He could feel the knot in his stomach begging to relieve itself at merely the thought of finding some form of happiness.

The next few days flew by, each one blending with the rest, but with the small pressing of hope for this new 'religion' thing he would try. Then the day finally arrived, Sunday morning. Both Madox and Kris got ready and dressed in nice outfits. Kris wore a floating red dress while Madox wore a nice shirt and black pants. This would be the first time they had dressed nicely in almost two years, the first time they did something together in three months, and the first time Kris left the house in two weeks.

They drove to Steward Street, finding a large red-bricked building with hundreds of cars stacked around it. The building had bright yellow letters spanning almost the entire 200-foot length of the front, displaying, 'First Church of Love' with a cross appended to the end. The building was square with beautiful flowers and plants blending with the smooth wooden doorway.

As they walked up, they were greeted by two men in nice suits, wearing plastic smiles like the girl from the other day.

"Love everyone."

"Love everyone."

They said one after the other as they held the door open for Madox and Kris to walk in. Walking in, Madox had a strange feeling in his gut. A feeling of unease, not knowing what he was getting himself into. Still, the glimmer of hope flickered in the back of his mind. *What if this is exactly what I need to escape my mundane, boring life?*

Walking inside, another set of bright letters displayed 'First Church of Love' sitting above what looked to be a receptionist desk. The room was slim with a tall roof, holding six different hallways numbered one through six, where Madox couldn't make out where they ended. The walls were white, covered in beautifully colored flowers and images of peace and love. People holding hands. The outline of a man kneeling down to hand a child a flower.

"Hi! Welcome to the First Church of Love! My name is Sally. Is there any way I can help you?" the cheerful woman from behind the desk asked with teeth so white she could be in a commercial. She was a black woman with a plump build, wearing a nicely knitted red sweater with a white cross in the middle. Her black hair, held up in a long braid, lay on her shoulder next to her rosy-cheeked face.

"Uh, yeah, we're first timers and came for church or something? Where should we-" Madox began before the woman cut him off.

"Yay! We love new people!" she shouted enthusiastically, shooting her hands up into the sky as if she had just won the lottery.

"So we have six different showings, go down hall one for rom-coms, hall two for comedy, hall three for football, hall four for sitcom TV, hall five for action, and hall six for news. The sermons are an hour long, so make sure to relax for at least an hour!"

The woman motioned cheerfully at all the different halls.

"Oh, can we watch the news? I haven't been keeping up to date with current events lately," Kris said, pulling Madox to Hall Six.

"Yeah, whatever," he agreed, knowing they wouldn't remember any of it anyway.

They walked into a black theater room, with rows of staggered chairs leading to a huge screen. There were around thirty others inside, all mesmerized by the screen. The two quickly found seats a few rows down and began watching, quickly becoming entranced by the screen themselves.

"Oh, yes, these little puppies are adorable!" the beautiful woman on the screen managed to say with four puppies surrounding her with licks and cuddles.

"Oh, they most certainly are!" the man next to her said, facing the same situation.

"So these puppies are now available in the new 'Puppy Playtime' line of memories, and let me tell you, Jeff, I most certainly cannot wait to get my hands on those memories!" the woman said as images and videos of the 'Puppy Playtime' memories ran across the screen.

Madox looked around the room, all the people watching with colorful smiles of glee on their faces. He could see the reflection of the screen in Kris's eyes as she seemed to fade outside this world. Suddenly, two men from off stage came and grabbed the puppies from the news reporters, leaving them laughing and giggling a few moments longer.

"Oh, so much fun! All you viewers better make sure to get your hands on some of these memories, they're a riot! But now we turn to our daily 'relative reality' reminder. So, to all you viewers out there, we want you to remember that when there's a problem, there's a memory to cover that! Any time you find yourself in an unpleasant situation or hear something not matching your own reality, make sure to cover that memory up with a new and better one! And don't be afraid to call the Memory Information Control Police, who are more than happy to help your reality be whatever you want! And remember, ignorance is bliss!" the man on the screen said like manna to his flock of followers.

"Ignorance is bliss," Kris let out under her breath without realizing.

The audience continued watching the news, displaying the same routine over and over. The news anchors would bring out some fun things to show the audience and advertise the line of memories associated with it. Then, after enough advertising, they would move to reminding the viewers to 'keep reality relative' and make sure to call the MPs. Madox knew it was all nothing but crap, yet couldn't manage to force his eyes to look away. The colors, the sounds, the happiness flowing from the screen seemed to encapsulate him, preventing any thoughts from flowing freely.

"Keep reality relative," Madox repeated unconsciously, just as he remembered in his childhood.

Around an hour passed, and suddenly the lights flicked on, and the screen turned off. Everyone turned around, getting out of their seats in unison like pigs marching to their troughs after hearing the dinner bell ring. Madox and Kris stood up and began walking with the crowd, blending in as best they could. Looking around, it seemed every person had a smile on their face, though Madox couldn't figure out why.

They marched back into the original room, all lined up to the front desk with Sally holding a box in her hand and an unwavering smile. There were people coming from each of the other halls, too, each just as happy as the ones from this room. They waited in line for around five minutes until eventually making it to the front, where Sally stood holding a box of cassettes.

"Here's this week's sermon! There's complimentary AMTs next to the exit doors if you need! Can't wait to see you next week!" she somehow smiled wider with a slight tilt of her head.

Madox reached in and grabbed two cassettes, both with the writing, 'Sunday Service' on the front. After noticing the line for the AMTs was even longer than the line for the cassettes, they decided to use their own AMT in the car. On their way outside, they noticed the people using the AMTs seemed different than before.

"Love everyone," an older woman said, taking off the AMT and wrapping her arms around her husband as they kissed passionately.

"Love everyone," a younger man shouted, taking off his AMT then his shirt, before kissing his woman as well.

They quickly noticed everyone around them slowly began to lose their clothes as the echoing of 'love everyone' bounced around the room. A spark of curiosity and excitement flickered between Madox and Kris. They rushed to see what all the commotion was about, briskly walking outside with the same two men holding open the door.

"Love everyone!"

"Love everyone!"

Like déjà vu, their voices echoed through Madox's ears. Quickly, they walked back to the car and got inside. Kris had the AMT on before Madox had the chance to sit down. She put the cassette in and set the time. A sudden flash came from the AMT. Kris leaned her head back against the seat and let her arms lose strength as they fell to her sides.

"You okay, Kris?" Madox asked, half-worried and half intrigued over what was in that memory.

"Love everyone," she moaned, leaving her jaw open as the words fell out of her mouth.

Madox was more intrigued than before. He had to see what was in that memory. She took off the AMT and placed it on Madox's lap, turning to him with eyes full of lust. Before he could put the headset on, Kris was on top of him, sucking his neck lightly as her hands explored his body.

Madox was able to reach around Kris and replace the headset's cassette, as he was more concerned with what he would find in the memory than anything Kris could do to him. He placed the headset on with the time set from one hour ago to the present. He took a deep breath, holding the AMT controller.

Flick

Bright white light covered an open area surrounded by large marble pillars of white and gold. Clouds were so thick and pure, surrounding the pillars and floor as though they themselves held up the entire world. A flock of white shadows sat directly above the open roof, singing a beautiful harmony of love and pleasure. The feel of a soft hand gently touching from beneath the cloud covering the floor.

"Come with us," the voice whispered.

Beneath the cloud lay hundreds of others, kissing and playing freely as their naked skin pressed together. A sense of euphoria flowing as all humanity lay peacefully, making love as a sign of unity and harmony. Pleasure surged through the glowing air, dissolving everything into warmth and light. The heat from the bodies evaporated the sins of the people as they touched one another freely.

"Love everyone!" a booming voice shouted from the heavens.

"Love everyone!" the crowd shouted back.

"Love everyone!" the voice boomed again.

"Love everyone!" the crowd shouted back as arms and heads looked to the heavens.

Tears of joy and pleasure fell freely like gold as the world made love to itself. Whispers of "Love everyone" muffled through the kissing of lips. Feelings so vivid and extreme, like the rush of a firework exploding on a perfect night.

"Love everyone!" the voice boomed once again.

"Love everyone," Madox whispered lightly, feeling lips softly pressing his neck as a single tear rolled down his cheek.

Love Everyone —
Naked bodies
Feeling good
Not reality
What does it make us?
Christianity?

CHAPTER 5

The sun rose beautifully as the tall, swaying pine trees seemed to bow to the sun in thanks for its warmth. Madox rose from his bed to the sound of his alarm as Kris lay asleep naked next to him. He knew he had to work, yet couldn't take the unfamiliar smile off his face. He could vividly remember everything that had happened the day before, and couldn't help but replay the images and feelings in his head over and over again. It was like the climactic ending of a show looping endlessly, as feelings of happiness and pleasure coiled in his mind.

Throughout Madox's life, his memories felt like the dull gray of winter — reliving the same mundane routine: mind-numbing TV in the evenings with splinter-filled, tedious jobs of dusting, dishwashing, and sweeping, during the day. Yet through the coarse dread of his life, a shot of color like a firework exploding in his mind seemed to have gone off, giving him a taste of happiness for the first time ever.

As he pulled on his pants and shirt, images of naked bodies lying next to one another formed joyously in his mind. The smooth-sounding choir and the touch of skin so real he couldn't help but close his eyes to try and re-live the moment.

"Love everyone," he whispered to himself, walking out the front door.

A few weeks passed, with Madox and Kris attending each service as they grew entranced by Christianity. The sermons were always similar, yet different. The same feelings of euphoria and joy tied together with the beautiful bodies and warmth. The choirs always sang beautifully as the preacher chanted his glorious tune of "love everyone." Yet the settings and people were always new.

One week, they were in a bright, warm cornfield, and each person had their own partner to play with as they lay comfortably in the endless field. Another week, they sat atop a snowy mountain, so quiet and beautiful, as the sun slowly crept over the horizon. Madox's favorite was when they all made love deep in the woods, untouched by the outside world, in their starry oasis.

Quickly, Madox not only found himself with memories of joy and happiness, but also discovered he could hold onto those feelings in the present. A smile became his signature facial expression as life filled with color. His dull life of gray seemed to have blown into a colorful array of beauty, forming into a lovely tapestry over the course of time itself.

As he drove to work, the joy of the services he had attended replayed in his head. He even enjoyed thinking of the time after the sermons with Kris, as he enjoyed that time more than he ever had before. After enough weeks, he even began to not overwrite his memories of Kris, which he always replaced to keep in line with Kris's reality of her being a woman and his own heterosexuality. His foot tapped and danced during the entire drive over as his smile continued to grow. As he walked into Mem-Co, the lady at the desk greeted him politely.

"Good morning, Mr. Rightly! Mr. Dayfell is waiting in the lab department for you, just head down this hall and to the left!" she said, pointing down the hall.

"Thank you! Love everyone!" Madox responded cheerfully.

Walking through the hallway and into the room filled with key tapping, his smile remained untouched. The signs on the walls — 'ignorance is bliss' and 'Mem-Co, where your dreams come true!' — gave him a sense of comfort in the unfamiliar room.

"Madox! Hey, I'm Selleck. You're with me," a man said, passing Madox from behind, giving him two pats on the back.

"Sounds good," Madox responded cheerfully as they walked to the set of black doors deep in the lab.

They quickly made it through the security procedures, with Selleck taking control of everything, allowing them to enter the next room. As Madox entered the room, his knees hit the floor as tears ran from his eyes, staring at the rows of children strapped to chairs. His mind raced as his belief in "love everyone" sank into his heart.

"I bet you're wondering what all this is. The cassette I gave you should explain most everything," Selleck said, handing him an AMT.

"It's only a ten-minute memory; you usually use the drive here to replace it with."

Madox took the AMT with shaky hands, taking out the cassette labeled 'For Madox' on the side and replacing it with the new one he was given. He turned the time to his drive over and put the device on. A quick flash of light sparked before taking the device off.

"How... how could we do this to them? We are supposed to love everyone..." Madox looked at Selleck through watery lenses.

"Are you alright? You've been acting weird these past couple of weeks with your, 'love everyone' bull crap. You didn't get into Christianity, did you? Oh fuck, how did I not see this before?" Selleck looked down, grabbing between his eyes. "Ok, let me just get it all out there. Your job is to keep these kids alive, so how about we not go through the whole 'morality' and 'love everyone' conversation. I can assure you there is nothing you can do for them, and the best way to 'love' them is to keep them alive. You got that?"

Madox's fingers twitched as tears continued slowly falling to the ground. Hours piled up like weights as Madox worked. The sounds of distant clanging of metal, along with the faint zaps of the children's helmets, filled the air. Madox worked silently just as he did every other day. A deep knot held tight in his stomach as he walked the endless corridors.

Yet, even through the pain and sadness, Madox held a glimmer of hope. The images of Sunday service ruffled through his mind, blocking out his thoughts and feelings of the children lying limp in their seats. Like a single plank out in the middle of the ocean during a thunderstorm, Madox had something to hold onto to keep him from drowning.

The hours flew by, with nothing but the thoughts of church and the fact that he could switch his memories out as soon as he left, holding him together. Even the suspiciously empty seat marked with the number '44934402' left him unfazed as the images of pleasure and comfort filled his mind.

At last, Madox's shift was over, and he left with a knotted stomach. Driving down the road, he saw a rustic gas station and swerved into the parking lot. Rushing inside, still trying to keep the images of the children blurred by the images of the Sunday service, his eyes shot straight to the shelf of cassettes next to the man at the cash register.

"You're in luck today," the cashier with a long beard cracked, grabbing a cassette off the shelf. "We got a few level threes today. They do come with ads, of course, but they'll be cheap as dirt compared to the regulars."

"Do I know you?" Madox responded, confused.

The man threw down a Mem-Caster on the table and put the cassette inside, "No, but I know you. Just look at this one."

Twitching, Madox grabbed the Mem-Caster and threw it on his head.

The black sky illuminated through the vibrant air. Neon signs filled with color warmed the cool bricks rising up the towering buildings. Reflections bounced from the puddles sprinkled throughout the black streets. A cigar rests tastefully, blowing into the endless night, walking along the sidewalk, holding the warm hand of a figure covered in sparkling red. They giggle as they pull past the crowds of blurs, smiling and laughing vividly through the fluorescent signs.

Neon hearts flash overhead as the figure continues into a building, flaring in lights and sounds. The man at the door knows the figure in red, laughing as he throws them a set of keys, and they continue deeper into the heart of the party. Walking into a large room, hundreds of people in bright colors dance energetically as bright lights flash all around. Music booms through the party, running its intoxicating beats through the people.

The figure in red finds an empty booth in the corner, seemingly empty to the world around.

A blurred smiling woman holding two sparkling drinks walks up, placing the drinks on the table, "Welcome to Night in the City, where the party never ends! This is where all your deepest desires come true! With a low entry fee of one hundred fifty dollars, you can pleasure yourself to all the wonderful opportunities this place holds. Some of the many things you can do include unlimited drinks, dancing, sex, and non-stop music. Every Friday, we host a mini-concert with some of your favorite singers! The entry fee costs an additional fifty dollars, but nothing compared to the limitless joy you will experience! And for all you lovers out there, we also provide any kind of sexual pleasures you desire, with additional payment, of course. But there is so much more, so make sure to always come back to Night in the City, where the party never ends!"

As the woman began walking away, the music seemed to slow down. Hands softly touch, as the lust-filled air steams over the figure in red. Their body pushes against the back of the booth, as their smooth skin feels delicious, sliding under their red dress. Softly, lips touch as hearts float all around.

"Alright, that's enough," the cashier ripped the Mem-Caster off Madox's head. "Do you want it? Only twenty dollars!"

Tapping along the floor, Madox looked over to the shelf of cassettes. The level ones and twos were cheap but boring. 'Lying awake in bed,' 'Night guard,' 'Petting a cat,' a few of the cheap memories marked on the front. The threes and fours were much better, but way out of his price range. 'Night in Vegas,' 'Trip to the Bahamas,' 'Sex Party,' were a few of the expensive cassettes read. 'Trip to Colorado' is a level four displayed in bold with a small mountain keychain attached to it.

"I'll take it," Madox groaned as his tear-stained eyes watched the cashier smile in glee.

"Terrific! That'll be twenty dollars," he placed the cassette on the table as Madox handed him the cash.

Madox swiped the cassette and quickly ran back outside to his car. Grabbing the AMT out of the passenger seat, he placed the cassette inside and put it on his head. Grabbing the remote, he made sure the time was set correctly.

Flick

Madox shot up like a rocket as his body began to tingle. His foot rested calmly on the floor while his mouth hung open, gasping for air.

"I gotta go back to Night in the City, that was amazing," he said to himself before driving back home.

Part Two

Birds chirped all around as Madox made his rounds to everyone in the auditorium, dragging Kris along with him. The black screen hung over like the endless sky on a cloudless night, as the lights twinkled like stars overhead. Madox's smile beamed half as bright as his voice, carrying "love everyone" to every face he could see.

"Madox! How's it goin'?" a familiar voice sang like a lute.

He turned to find Ralph standing pleasantly, with Julia holding his arm at his side.

"It's going great! Love everyone!" Madox responded with equal joy in his voice.

"It's good to see you!" Kris stepped in.

"I'm glad to hear it, and it's good to see ya too, Kris! Say, you seem in an awfully good mood there, Madox."

"Have you heard of Christianity? It's wonderful! I have never felt so amazing in my life! It's full of love, peace, and unity! You should join us Sunday!" Madox couldn't contain his excitement.

"Well, that just sounds spectacular, but unfortunately, Sundays are our Muslim get-togethers where we go out into nature for a while. We just love nature, and we look forward to it every week. Last week we went to... Oh, where was it, Julia?"

"We went down to Florida to the world's largest butterfly park!" she giggled.

"Oh yes, of course! It was wonderful with all these beautiful critters flying all around, you'll just have to see it. If you'd ever like to join us, you're sure more than welcome!

Just as Ralph finished talking, the lights dimmed, and the crowd made their way to their seats.

"Maybe one of these weeks I will, great seeing you though! Love everyone!" Madox waved as he and Kris walked back to their seats.

Sitting in their seats, the screen flicked on as the movie played. Colors flashed over the crowd as they laughed and cried in unison. Sounds boomed through the speakers, loud enough to cover any thought that might appear.

While watching, he noticed a woman with red hair a few rows in front of him. He couldn't help but notice her beauty as her eyes poured into the screen. *I should make sure she feels love, too.*

An hour and a half whizzed by, with a sudden flash of the lights turning back on. Madox held his soft smile on his face as the people in black made their way down the aisles, passing the boxes of AMTs down the rows. As the box made its way down Madox's row, the crowd shouted and cheered.

"I LOVE MEM-CO!"

"YEAH! MEM-CO!"

"THANK YOU, DR. VELTIK! THANK YOU, MEM-CO!"

The box reached Kris, who put the AMT on without hesitation.

Flick

Tears rolled down her face as she shouted in joy, "YES! GO MEM-CO!"

Intrigued with what the memory could possibly be, Madox threw his AMT on.

Flick

Rot and gunpowder flew rank in the air as gray clouds covered the sky. The sounds of explosions and bullets zipping overhead were engraved into the soldiers' ears, even after the last bullet was fired. Silence and frost overtook the land as bodies scattered across the open field, riddled with trenches and bones. Frost nips at fingers as the heavy uniform and gun pull weak knees to the ground. A man sobbing in the distance, another frozen in shock as his arm sits half a mile away from his emptied body.

"Listen here, men!" A beefy man wearing a suit without blemish stood high on a hill, speaking to the entire army. "My name is Dr. Veltik. I know the fight was long and hard, but we managed to come out victorious. I want all of you to remember this day. Remember this day when remembering pain caused so much death and destruction. Remember this day, when tasked with choosing peace over anger. Remember this day as the result of not choosing Mem-Co. The cost was great, but our freedom is worth the payment."

All the men began gathering around, listening to him as tears ceased. The clouds parted, sending a bright beam of warm sun to pour over Veltik as he continued his speech.

"You all have the choice to choose peace over death. I promise you this: as long as you stay with Mem-Co, this suffering will never happen again. Choosing to remember over pain will lead to a peaceful world of sunshine. So stand with me!" he shouted as the crowd around him cried tears of joy. "Stand with me in choosing life! Stand with me in choosing freedom from suffering! Stand with me in choosing Mem-Co! Veltik shouted, raising his gun to the air as the crowd cheered with him.

"YEAH MEM-CO!"

Part Three

Weeks rolled into months as the same routine carved its way into stone. Madox was now a fully-fledged Christian, advocating "love everyone" to every person he saw. Each week, he would return to Sunday service as though they were handing him the bread of life itself.

One week, as Madox and Kris walked into church, a different woman stood behind the counter. She was plump with dark skin and tightly curled hair, holding a large white smile on her face. As they began walking down hall number three, she stopped them in their tracks.

"Hey! Do you have a moment to talk?" the woman asked.

"Of course! What is it?" Madox responded enthusiastically.

"Well, we are actually going to be having a mission trip in a few weeks, and we were just wondering if you would like to participate!"

"What's that?" Madox asked, intrigued.

"Well, part of being a Christian and loving everyone means we have to sometimes go out and help others and show the love of Christians to the world! So, we are having a group of people go down to Africa for a week to help the natives living in high poverty areas find out what love really is!"

Without hesitation, Madox blurted, "Yes, I'd love to show more people love! Love everyone!"

"Amazing! We'll mark you down right here," the woman said, pulling a clipboard from behind the counter.

"You go ahead and do that without me, I'm just fine at home, thanks," Kris denied the clipboard as Madox tried to pass it to her.

"Yes, and that's just fine too! You all have a good rest of your day! And I'll be seeing you in a few weeks! My name is Danyella, by the way," she held out her hand.

"Madox," he responded with a large smile, shaking her hand vigorously.

The excitement of the mission trip fluttered in his mind as the thought of showing love to people around the world felt like a dream. The weeks stretched on as his mind wrapped around what all they would be doing in Africa. He had only been to Africa one other time on a three-week safari vacation alone. He could remember the smells, animals, sounds, and trees. His tongue tingled as he remembered the taste of the fresh stew he had sitting in the shade of a Baobab tree as a flock of gazelles stomped by in the distance.

A few days before the trip, Denis sat in their usual booth at 'A Drink to Remember.' The bright lighting covered the joyful air as the bartender stood on the phone behind the ragged wooden countertop. Denis downed another beer, adding the empty bottle to his collection sitting cold on the table. Madox walked in and sat quietly next to him, holding an unnatural smile on his face.

"What's up with you? And what's with that weird grin on your face?" Denis asked as though Madox had blood pouring from his forehead.

"I have some exciting news for you that I've been waiting to share. I joined Christianity, and I'm going on a mission trip in a few weeks! Madox spoke joyfully like a child speaking to their parent.

Denis took a moment, seemingly unfazed by what he had said, as his face froze. His eyes were dull as he looked Madox up and down. He took a long, silent breath in and out before turning to the bartender.

"Another," he said, setting his elbows on the table and putting his hands together. "Christianity, you say? A mission trip? Sorry, but I think that's all horse shit."

Madox's eye twitched as his smile kept glued to his face, "Horse-? What are you talking about? Christianity is amazing, and I definitely think you should try it! I'd love if you came with me Sunday to church, it would be the most incredible thing you've ever experienced!" his eyes tingled with excitement.

The bartender finished his call and brought Denis another beer, which he downed as soon as the glass touched his lips.

"You don't say? What is it that you guys say all the time? Love people or something?" Denis asked, keeping his eyes on the liquor case behind the bar counter.

"Love everyone! And that's exactly what we do! We love everyone! It's like Christianity has brought the world together in peace and love!" Madox continued in his same joyful voice.

"Get out of there, Madox. You don't want anything to do with them..." Denis said coldly.

Madox's face dropped as his head spun around. "What are you talking about? This is the best thing that's ever happened to me! I'm happy now! Can't you see that?" Madox became angry.

"It's all shit, and the sooner you leave, the better," Denis shot back just as cold, keeping his eyes behind the table.

Madox could feel his heart pound as his breath shot from his ears, "Fine! Be like that! Love everyone!" he stormed out of the diner, fuming without a glance from Denis.

"The nerve of him! He doesn't know what he's talking about! I am finally happy, and he just says it's shit!" Madox shouted in his car, driving home. "I don't need him. I just need Christianity. Yeah, that's all I need."

His veins cooled as his breath deepened, "Love everyone..."

A few weeks rolled by, and the day came when they would be leaving for Africa. Madox shot out of bed with excitement, jumping through his fingers. He already had his three briefcases filled with clothes and bathroom supplies that he knew he would be needing on his week-long adventure. He happily drove to church and met up with a group of about fifty others, just as excited as he was.

"-member there was this little adorable girl with the cutest little face and eyes, and I gave her a sucker, and her eyes just lit up because it was the first time she had ever had candy in her life! It was the most wholesome, amazing thing I have ever experienced," Madox caught the end of a woman describing one of the past mission trips she went on.

"Alright, everyone, gather round!" Danyella shouted as everyone huddled around. "How's everyone doing!"

The crowd cheered, full of energy.

"I know you are all probably very excited to be going to Africa, but there are just a few things we need to discuss before leaving, okay!" she said, holding a clipboard.

The first thing she did was call roll, finding all sixty-one people were here and accounted for. Then she began handing out plane tickets and other items they may need for the trip. Lastly, she handed them AMTs and cassettes labeled 'Africa Mission Trip.' Madox quickly used the cassette, immediately remembering all the rules of travel that could be summed up to 'do what you are told' and 'be loving to everyone.' Madox also remembered their quick Swahili lesson to allow for basic conversation with the natives.

Finally, they all boarded onto a few buses and headed for the airport, where Madox could barely contain his excitement as he shouted, "Love everyone," walking through the bus door. Driving over, Madox felt excitement bubbling in his stomach. He had never experienced such joy and fulfillment in his life. *Christianity is everything I ever needed. I can't wait to share it with everyone!*

Arriving at the airport, the group passed through security and boarded the plane as quickly as they could. The plane ride was seventeen hours long, but Madox didn't mind as the screen on the backside of the seat in front of him played the news the whole ride over. 'Puppy playtime' was now on its twenty-third cassette after becoming a hit, with many new cassettes Madox had never heard about.

Eventually, the plane landed, and they were finally in Africa. Madox felt like a champagne glass about to explode from excitement. It was completely dark out as they arrived at 1:23 AM. The group quickly grabbed their bags and left the airport, following Danyella to a group of black jeeps guarded by ten memory police in black padded suits.

"Don't worry, everyone, they are just here to protect us from any wild animals and keep us safe. Let's all hop in to head to camp, we have a big day tomorrow!" Danyella cheered as they climbed into the jeeps.

Almost everyone had fallen asleep during the drive to the camp about two hours away. Madox kept awake, looking at the beautiful night sky and stars he had never seen. The trees and dirt looked the same as the cool wind blowing through his hair made him feel as though he had never left home. In the distance, he could see plateaus and rivers formed so beautifully across the silent horizon.

"Love everyone," Madox spoke lightly to himself, ready to give the world his love.

They arrived at the camp sitting just outside a city of clay and brick houses. Multiple large white tents sat next to one another as the only light came from the flashlights Danyella gave them back at the church.

"Alright, everyone, this is our home for the next week! Let's all get settled in and get some rest!" Danyella shouted, waking up all the sleeping passengers.

Slowly, all the sleeping zombies made their way out of the jeeps and into one of the white tents filled with bunk beds. Madox settled into one of the lower beds, and everyone quickly fell asleep, excited to start the next day.

The sun slowly filled the tent as the morning air drifted through with the breeze.

"Alright, time to get up, everyone! We have lots to do!" Danyella shouted, waking everyone up around eight.

Madox was tired, but his excitement for the day overwhelmed his body. *I can't wait to help and love everyone!*

They all ate breakfast consisting of porridge and fruit, which Madox wasn't the biggest fan of, but knew it was part of African culture and blew it off. After breakfast, Danyella broke them all into groups to do different tasks. Group one was supposed to go out and help bring people to camp for love, group two's job was to give love, and group three's job was post-love.

Luckily, Madox made it into group two, where he would be giving love to the people. After splitting into groups, Danyella took Madox and the rest of the people in group two to a nearby tent and began explaining their job.

"So you all get the privilege of giving love to people! This is the most beautiful and crucial part of loving people," she began before holding up an AMT. "You see, most of these people have lived hard and difficult lives of poverty. Most have watched friends and family die from disease and malnutrition. As such, you all will be giving special AMTs and cassettes, and your job is to give them memories of a new and wonderful life! Not of death and pain, but of happiness and love! So you will all have your own tent, and group one will bring people for you to give love to. Then, once you have given them love, these special AMTs will put them to sleep in order to preserve the reality of them never having lived in poverty. So they will fall asleep and wake up in a warm bed with a new, happy life! So when they do fall asleep, you will place them on the bed stationed in your room for group three to come pick up and take them to their new home," she then went on to explain how they should talk to the people, and the best way to show love to them, even if they didn't understand one another completely. "Any questions?"

A knot formed in Madox's stomach. "Wait, so we're replacing their entire lives? Isn't that wrong? I thought we would be giving them food and water or things like that," Madox asked.

"Food and water are temporary, but memories are forever! It is much more beneficial to them that we replace their memories to help erase the awful things of their past. And afterwards, we will definitely give them all the food and water they need," Danyella explained with her white teeth shining brightly on her face.

"Yeah, I guess you're right," Madox agreed, despite his foot anxiously tapping the ground.

She then began assigning tents to each person, going down the line until eventually reaching Madox's tent.

"And here you are!" she said, walking into the tent. "The AMT and cassettes are right there, and if you need anything, I'll be making rounds, alright!" she said, leaving out the opposite side of the tent.

Madox could feel his stomach swirl from anticipation and excitement. *How will these people react? What do I say to them? What if I do something wrong?* His head spun until, suddenly, a sound came from the flapping of the white curtain doors.

An older gentleman with gray frizzy hair and dark brown skin walked in, holding a cane in his hand. His face wrinkled to where his mouth formed a permanent frown, as his neck shot from his shoulders. He wore a colorfully woven cloth covering his entire body while a rough brown stick held him up.

"Hi," Madox shouted by accident. "My name is Madox, what's yours?" he asked, trying to speak in his language while holding out his hand.

The man seemed unfazed, continuing to walk until stopping in the center of the room. Madox was scared and confused; he didn't know what to do or if the man could even understand him. He walked over to the bed and patted it.

"Come have a seat, I have something for you!" Madox said cheerfully, holding the best smile he could.

The man glanced at the bed, then stared Madox in the eyes. Suddenly, he walked over and sat down, holding the stick to the floor as his back stood up straight on the bed. Madox quickly grabbed the AMT and cassette.

"You put it on like this," Madox demonstrated how to put the AMT on.

The man looked at the device as though it were a new scientific discovery. Eventually, he put it on, and Madox put the cassette in.

"Alright, ready? In three, two..."

Flick

Madox hit the remote, sending a flash from the AMT, sending the older man's body limp onto the bed.

He's just asleep, that's just how these special AMTs work. Kinda scary though. Madox laid the man's limp body on the bed, taking off the AMT. The knot in his stomach grew tighter as he looked at the man lying there like a statue. Soon, a set of two people in white hazmat suits walked in from the opposite entrance, Madox and the older man who entered from there. They picked up the man and took him back through the mysterious white flapped doorway.

Soon, another person walked in, a young girl, and Madox did the same thing. Repeatedly, people began piling in as Madox continued giving love to each and every one of them. There were young boys and girls, some older, all scrawny as though they hadn't eaten in days. The thought of giving all these people an incredible new home fought against the nausea in his stomach as a smile grew on his face.

As the sky shone brighter, the sun melted the air. Madox couldn't keep track of the number of people he gave love to, as they continued to flood into his tent like clockwork. Each hour, Madox noticed the sound of a truck leaving and coming back to the tents. Still, he was too busy to think about it. Eventually, Danyella walked in from the same door the people in the white suits came in from.

"Hey, just checking in, you doing alright?" she asked kindly.

"Yeah, but where are those trucks going?" he asked.

"Oh, that's just our guys taking these people to our facilities, ensuring each one wakes up to an amazing new life with amazing new memories. I promise you are doing amazing work, and we will take care of these people to our fullest capabilities," Danyella answered quickly with a smile on her face.

"Yeah, that makes sense, thanks!" Madox replied, feeling his anxiousness begin to fade.

A few hours passed as Madox gave love to an endless number of people. To him, each person who entered was a person he would save. A person in need of love and peace, away from the stench of pain, suffering, and death. *What an amazing gift to be able to love others and bless them with new, amazing lives!*

As the sun crawled back down the sky, Danyella came back, this time through the front flaps of the tent, holding the hand of a boy who couldn't have been over the age of six.

"This is Dakarai, he's your last one for today," Danyella said happily, leading the boy over to the bed.

He was small and scrawny, as though he might have died in the next few days. His skin was smooth and dark black with short, fuzzy black hair. He had wide, curious eyes and a smile brighter than anyone he had seen that day.

"He is very excited to be getting love, and I'm excited for him too. The village elders told me the rest of his family had died of malnutrition, and he doesn't have long. He watched his friends and family die, but we get to change that for him. We get to give him peace and love!" she said excitedly.

Both sorrow and happiness mixed in Madox's heart as he put the device on his head. He could see his smile shining brightly even through living such a hard life.

Flick

The boy's smile vanished as his limp body hit the bed. Madox took a deep sigh, knowing this was the right thing to do.

"Alright, grab his body, you have one more thing you have to do before you're done for the day," Danyella said, walking through the exit door.

Something in the way Danyella spoke grew the knot back in Madox's stomach, which swirled as he picked up the boy's limp body and walked through the white flapped door. He followed Danyella, carrying the boy to a large truck, filled with hundreds of native bodies stacked on top of one another. Madox's stomach seemed to sink to the floor as fear entered his veins.

"What is this? This can't be right? Why are we putting them in trucks like this?" Madox asked, confused.

"Throw the boy in the back and get in the truck," Danyella spoke coldly.

He threw him in the back and walked to the front of the truck. Danyella sat in the driver's seat while Madox sat in the passenger seat. His foot tapped furiously across the floor as questions swirled through his head.

"Danyella, what is going on? This ca-"

"Shut up, I'll explain everything once we get there," she cut him off in a deathly tone.

Madox's mouth zipped shut as the car moved forward. After around fifteen minutes of silent driving, Madox saw clouds of smoke in the distance, multiplying the fear and questions in his brain. Another few minutes passed, and they arrived at the smoke, surrounded by a large white tent like the one they had been in.

Parking the car, Danyella told Madox to get out and help her. Stepping outside the truck, Madox gagged at the crisp, rotting air filling his nostrils. *What the fuck is that?* Madox froze with fear, forcing him to do as he was told. He walked around the back of the car and picked up the same child he had just thrown into the truck. *There has to be a perfectly good explanation for whatever's in there. It will all be alright.*

They walked over to a white flapped door in the tent as Madox's entire body screamed in fear. Then, his body filled with dread as he saw what was on the other side. Hundreds of bodies lay in piles as people in white hazmat suits tossed their limp corpses on top of one another. The rotting smell of smoke funneled from the rolling hills as the men poured flame-throwers and gasoline over the horrific sight.

"Just throw him on any of the piles, and make sure to take the AMT off him," Danyella said casually, waving her hand at the piles as she continued to walk through the camp.

Madox could feel his hands shake as tears rolled from his eyes. Instantly, he knew what he had done to this poor boy. In his mind, the image of the boy's smiling face became a knife to his throat.

"Wait," Madox cried, halting Danyella in her tracks. "Why? Why are you doing this? I thought we were here to help them; we are supposed to love everyone."

Danyella turned around and walked back to Madox, "Why? Why wouldn't we? We are helping them. We're getting rid of their pain and suffering. It's better for them to die like this than to keep living as they were. At least we give them peace when they die. Like I said, this kid had to watch his friends and family die from malnutrition, and he would have died too if we hadn't come along. And worse, he would have died knowing it was all for nothing. Do you really want that for these poor children? To let them die knowing all their suffering and pain was for nothing?"

"Of course not!" Madox shot back angrily through dried tears. "I wanted to help these children and give them a better life! Why couldn't we take them back with us, or bring food here to them! There is no need to kill them all! There is no need for any of this!"

"Bring them back with us? Bring them food? Are you hearing yourself? First, the children over the age of two can't go back with us. We tried talking to Mem-Co, but apparently, they are too old as Mem-Co only takes infants. And it's not like anyone wants to take care of these disgusting brats. Nobody even knows how to take care of kids. And what would bringing them food do? Prolong their suffering? Even if they lived to be adults, there would be no future for them. They would continue to watch their friends and family die, and if they somehow had kids, they would be left in the same cruel world. It's an endless cycle of pain and suffering trying to help these people. It's far better for them to die happy than continue to live in suffering. This way, we can give them a humane, peaceful death with memories of an amazing life well lived. I mean, it's no different than hospitals. It's better to die peacefully than live with terminal cancer for the rest of your short life. Most people can't handle the fact that they are going to die; luckily, that's what we are here for. We make death peaceful," she shot back, unfazed, as though trying to shoot a bullet through Madox's head.

"But can't we just change their memories? Make them able to adapt to our world? Not punish them for their poverty or sickness?" Madox fought back.

"Madox, we can't take hundreds of thousands of people from poor countries and just stick them into society, even if we did give them memories to fit in. We don't have the food, space, money, or resources to support them. The problem here isn't poverty; it's overpopulation, and we are the solution to both those who are chosen for love and those profiting from it. If we keep this up, someday there will be no more poverty or pain. Only harmony and happiness with everyone loving one another in perfect unity. This is just one step that must be taken to reach perfect love and unity in society. It doesn't even matter, you'll just expunge this memory like everyone else," her face untouched by the crack of fire and smell of corpses only a few feet away.

"Well—well, what if I choose to remember, what if I wanted to know and tell everyone how awful Christianity really is," Madox continued with fire burning in his chest.

"You and I both know we won't let you remember anything here. But let's be honest, the pain of knowing is much worse than the peace of ignorance; you couldn't keep yourself from replacing this memory if you wanted to. 'Ignorance is bliss,' she spoke as though debating with satan himself. "Anyway, your last job here is to help take care of the burnt bodies. There are hazmat suits in the tent over there, and Tony will tell you what to do. The sooner you get the job done, the sooner you can put that little slop-filled mind of yours at ease, so chop-chop."

Danyella walked off once again, pointing to a nearby tent, before walking into a large white tent with the entrance protected by two memory police. Madox stood frozen, holding the boy's body as tears rolled from his eyes.

"Fuck me," he said out loud, throwing his corpse onto the pile with all the others as vomit curled up his throat.

He quickly put on his suit and found Tony, who handed him a shovel. Madox's last job was to move the ashes of the burnt bodies into trucks to be shipped off and dumped into a pit three miles down the road.

The hot sun rolled across the sky as Madox spent hours shoveling up the new friends he had just made. His body was covered in sweat as the smell of ash, rot, and vomit he had thrown up three times smoldered in the heat. His veins burned in anger as the images of the crisp bodies collided with Dakarai's innocent face.

He noticed all of the other people held tears and pain in their eyes. He watched a group of three of them try to break into the tent Danyella disappeared into in hopes of finding an AMT. Unfortunately, the memory police beat them until they got back to work. Telling them they would get their memories erased once their job was complete.

After two long hours, the last of the ashes were shipped off, and a voice rang from Danyella's tent, "Good work today, everyone! Please make your way to the East Tent for memory replacements!"

Within seconds, the entire force of white hazmats was lined in perfect fashion to the East Tent. Madox stood in the slowly moving line as each person disappeared in the white folds of the tent. He could hear small whimpers and cries as he stood in line. All the others were fated to the same horrible reality as him. Madox kept his head to the ground as images of bodies, ash, and the boy's smile stapled to his brain. Even the thought of Denis — how he warned him of Christianity, and how he should have listened, flickered through his brain.

"I can't take it anymore!" a woman's voice came from behind him as a white suit dashed by.

"Stop that, get back in line!" one of the memory police shouted at her, holding his baton over his head.

She dropped to the floor, holding her hands to the sky to protect herself as he began beating her with his baton.

Madox stood silently on the side with boiling veins, watching this man beat an innocent woman. Her eyes bubbled with tears as the man continued to scream at her. To Madox, it felt like what they did to these innocent people, beating them on the ground, even though they were not going to hurt anyone. Images of Dakarai began to replace the woman as Madox himself replaced the officer. His hands gripped into fists tighter with each punch.

"Love everyone," Madox whispered to himself, walking out of the line. "Stop that! She's had enough!" Madox shouted as all eyes turned to him.

The man looked over in his black mask and goggles, "You want some of this too?" he asked, pointing to Madox.

Madox took a deep breath as his fists rose from his sides-"I'm so sorry for my friend here, officer, he didn't mean you any disrespect," a man came from behind, holding Madox's arms down.

"I think what he was trying to say is she can't take any more beatings. We still have four days left of this trip, so you wouldn't want her to be unable to work, do you? And not to mention, it would be hard to explain all the bruises and broken bones after getting her memories replaced, right? You wouldn't want her reality to be altered because you took her beating a little too far, would you?" The man talked in a smooth, calm voice.

The officer held his baton for a moment, looking at both Madox and the man.

"Fine! You get back in line!" he shouted at the woman, who quickly ran back in line full of tears. "And you two better watch it!" he shouted before walking back to his position near the tent.

Madox and the man walked back in line. The man was short with black hair and a baby-looking face.

"Cover me," the man said, hiding behind Madox as he began to take off his shoe.

"What? Who are you? What are you doing?" Madox asked, confused as the line continued to move forward.

"Does it matter if I explain anything? You're not going to remember in a few minutes anyway. Just tell me your name," he said, finally taking off his shoe and pulling out a black marker.

Madox's eyes lit in terror as he realized what it was, "You can't have that here! Who knows what they'll do to us! You heard what he said!"

Madox began flipping around his shoulders to make sure nobody could see.

"Just tell me your name, and I'll put it up," the man said calmly.

"Madox! Madox Rightly! Now put that away!"

He quickly pulled down his sock as he lifted his foot to his chest as far as he could, somehow standing in line perfectly balanced. On the bottom of his foot, he wrote, 'Madox Rightly' as best he could, before quickly putting his sock and shoe back on, and hiding the marker in his boot.

"What was that all about! You're insane!" Madox tried not to shout through his anger and confusion.

"See you when this is all over," the man said quietly before walking to the back of the line.

Madox's mind raced as questions fluttered like tiny rocks in a sandstorm. *Who was that man? What did he want? Why did he help me?* Yet, as each person walked into the tent, his boiling blood began to cool, realizing what the man said was true. It doesn't matter; he won't remember soon anyway.

The hot sun beat down as his thoughts transferred back to all the horrific things he had done. Even the thoughts of the church served little solace to his broken spirit. The line moved forward as the bodies sagged to get their slop from the warden. Eventually, it was Madox's turn through the white flaps of the tent. Walking into a small white room with a dirt floor, Danyella and an AMT sat in seats across from one another. In Madox's eyes, the AMT looked more like an apple of gold than a blanket over reality.

"Please, sit, the cassette is already inside," she said, waving to the AMT.

Madox picked the device up and sat down. Hurriedly, he placed the device on his head and turned it on as swiftly as possible.

Flick

Sunshine spoke as the trees whispered through the soft breeze. Kids in ripped clothing laugh as they dance in circles, singing songs of love and joy. Hands holding food, water, and toys, giving smiles to the innocent faces. A hollowed image of an older woman with a wrinkled face and decayed smile, as a conversation finds laughter through her forgotten stories. The hot sun poured sweat as bricks stacked on one another to form a school for the children now wearing their new bright clothing.

"Love everyone," the children sing as the cooks finish their dinner of roasted ham and chocolate cake.

Walking into the white tent, a young man walks up with thanks and praise as the day is finished, "You have saved us all! Thank you for every-thing you have done! Love everyone!"

"Love everyone," Madox said before taking off the AMT.

"How do you feel? How was your first day of the mission trip?" Danyella asked politely.

"It was amazing, I can't wait to start again tomorrow!" Madox responded enthusiastically. "Love everyone!"

CHAPTER 6

"We built schools and houses for all the people there. We provided them lots of food and water, and I learned lots of their fun dances and songs. I got to listen to the elders' stories of when they were young and how much we are changing their lives for the better. I got to show so much love to these kids and people! It was the most wonderful, best experience in the world!" Madox rattled off without a moment of breath.

"That sounds great, honey," Kris said tonelessly, lying on the couch with her mem-caster strapped to her face.

A smile strapped to Madox's face as he sat silently next to her, running his mind through all the colorful and happy memories of the mission trip. He could see the buildings they had built and how big and life-changing they were. He could smell the stew and flowers a little girl had brought to him. He could feel the soft hands of the children as he held them, singing in circles of dance. He could hear the sound of their sweet voices as they sang innocently across the beautiful scenery.

"I can't wait to go on another mission trip," Madox said, staring into the wall as his mind played on repeat like a rerun of a TV show.

That next Sunday, Madox was overly ecstatic to go back to church and tell everyone about the wonderful experiences he had. Walking in with Kris, he noticed lots of others in the main lobby, sharing their stories of the mission trip.

"Oh, Madox! We're so glad you're here! We're just going around telling everyone about our experiences on the mission trip and trying to get others to sign up for the next one," Danyella smiled lovingly.

Madox had to contain his body from exploding with joy as a group of people looked at him, ready to listen to his stories.

"It was incredible! I highly recommend going, it's so fulfilling and makes you feel so wonderful inside! Can I sign up for the next one?" Madox asked Danyella with starry eyes.

"Of course!" she said, handing over a clipboard for Madox to sign.

He quickly signed it and handed it back over, beginning to tell a group of about five-six smiling people all the adventures of love and happiness he went on during the trip.

"Hey, so your name is Madox?" A man grabbed him by the shoulder from behind while Madox was midway through a story.

Madox turned around to find a short man with a baby-looking face dressed in a nice red suit.

"Uh, yeah, that's me. Who are you?" Madox asked, confused.

"My name is Joshua, meet me in auditorium three after everyone is gone. And don't take the sermon yet," the man said ominously before walking away.

"Wait-what? Why? What do you need me for?" Madox asked as Joshua began walking away.

"I can't say anything here and now, just meet me there after everyone leaves, and come alone," he slipped into the crowd before Madox could continue to question him.

A knot formed in his stomach as anxiety about what the man could possibly want from him boiled in his brain. He turned around and finished his story, debating in the back of his mind whether to call the memory police or not. But, through his lovingly joyful spirit, he decided to see what the man had to say before he did anything rash.

The crowd eventually made their way into the auditoriums, where Madox and Kris decided on Hall Three this week. They watched the normal Sunday morning football, with the Good Guys winning 47-11. Kris wasn't a huge fan of football, but knowing she would remember something much better made the watching bearable.

Eventually, the time came when everyone got up and left. However, as everyone stood up, Madox stayed seated.

"What are you doing? It's time to get the sermon," Kris pulled on his arm, trying to get him out of the door.

"You go on without me. I'll catch up in a second," Madox responded shakily.

"Suit yourself," Kris left without a hitch.

Soon, Madox found himself sitting alone in the dark room. He waited five minutes before he noticed a warm light illuminate behind the screen. He stood up and began walking down the aisles until reaching the flat concrete wall holding the still vinyl screen.

"Hey, over here!" a whisper came from the right wall.

He looked over to see an unfamiliar face peeking out of a part of the black wall pushed in like a door. Madox's curiosity skyrocketed as the man waved him inside the secret room. Cautiously, Madox followed the man into a dark, black hall, as the only light was a small lantern held by the man. The left wall was smooth black concrete, connected to the auditorium, while the roof, floor, and left wall were made of decayed rough bricks of red and brown, with spiderwebs hanging down every corner.

They walked about ten feet before finding their way into a room filled with four other people sitting in a circular shape, including Joshua from earlier. The room was small with the same feeling as the hall, with the left side wall sitting directly behind the screen from the auditorium. There was a single warm light hanging naked from the ceiling, and a dangling string of silver spheres hung beside it. They all sat in scrawny chairs holding chipped paint and spider webs with two empty seats next to Joshua.

"Please have a seat," Joshua said, patting the seat next to him with a faint smile.

Carefully, Madox sat down, looking at all the mixed smiles glued to the others' faces.

"So, what's all this about?" Madox asked, looking at Joshua.

They all looked at each other silently, as though debating whether to answer Madox's question or not.

"We brought you here because we wanted to share something with you," Joshua began slowly. "We wanted to show you true Christianity..."

"I already know true Christianity, love everyone," Madox spun his head around the room.

"No-no," Joshua declined. "I mean true Christianity. Christians are called to love everyone, but that's not all being a Christian is," he spoke softly, trying to help Madox understand.

Madox could feel his brain split in two. One half curious as to what they had to say, the other seconds away from calling the memory police. Yet, the thought of what Denis had said rang in his mind. *'Get out while you can', 'It's all shit', was this what he was talking about? Is what they are going to tell me what Christianity truly is?*

"I can see this is a lot for you to take in, so we will stop, and maybe you can come back next week if you're ready," Joshua said with a defeated smile.

"Yeah, yeah, just let me think about this for a bit," Madox said as his mind wandered.

"Just please, please remember us," Joshua spoke with a weight to his voice.

That phrase alone was enough to call the memory police. Yet, for some reason, Madox didn't. They quietly let Madox out the way he came in, telling him to love everyone as they shut the secret door behind him. He walked out of the auditorium and found Kris, who had already remembered the sermon.

"Don't worry, I got a sermon for you. Let's get to the car so you can remember, it's so beautiful this week," she told him, handing him a cassette as she began pulling his arm out the door.

They quickly made it to the car, where Kris quickly got in on the passenger's side. But just outside the door, Madox stood with the door closed. He held the cassette in his hands, staring at it. 'Sunday Service' screamed in tiny black letters as thoughts and feelings of past services played with his mind. Still, for some reason, he couldn't get the feeling that something was off. *What were Denis and Joshua talking about? Should I just not remember all of it so I can be happy?*

"Ignorance is bliss," he whispered to himself. "But is bliss worth ignorance?"

He froze in shock at the sound of his own thought. Like opening a door without knocking to find something you would rather never see. He broke, realizing he had trailed too far off in his head. Then, like a runaway convict, he got in the car and slapped on his AMT. Then, just before using his remote, the words Joshua spoke came back to him.

'Just please, please remember us,' like gas on a fire, this phrase burned in his head.

"I've got to go do something first," Madox said, throwing the AMT into the back seat.

"Wait, what? What do you have to do?" Kris became upset and confused.

"It's nothing, I'm going to drop you off at home, and I'm not sure when I'll be back," Madox began driving home.

"Fine, see if I care," Kris flipped to face her body away from Madox.

He dropped her off at home and began speeding down the road. Soon, he reached a large white building with a gold dome roof and large white engraved pillars and walls. The building was complex, down to the finest of details of the carved spiral lions engraved in the walls. Atop the front pillars at the front of the building read, 'Charleston Memorial Library' in engraved white letters.

Madox parked and found his way to the large front doors made of marble and glass. Walking in, he was greeted by an enormous room filled with hundreds of shelves containing hundreds of cassettes. The room was luminously lit, with large windows spanning each wall, and bright white lights spewing from the ceiling. There were also multiple people fingering through boxes, as well as sitting in the TV area near the center of the room.

Madox walked up to the librarian, looking through boxes of cassettes at her large wooden desk. She had long blond hair with circular glasses, and couldn't have been over the age of 25. On her desk sat a small red sign reading, 'Learn the fun and fast way with Mem-Co!'

"Hi, do you all have anything about Christianity here?" Madox asked.

"Oh yeah, I think so, try the 'C' aisle that way," she pointed across the room.

Madox swiftly made his way over and began looking through boxes of cassettes to find anything that had to do with Christianity. He flipped through the cassettes, reading the names written on the front: 'Counting On Mem-Co', 'Cool Birds', 'Cactus's from around the world', and 'Cake for dinner.' Then, he found something, 'Christianity for Beginners.'

He took the cassette back to the librarian and handed it to her.

"Oh, glad you found what you are looking for," she said, scanning the barcode on the back. "This is an hour and twenty-five minutes, and costs nine dollars and thirty-four cents."

Madox pulled out his wallet and handed the money to the girl before taking the cassette.

"Have a nice day!" she waved as Madox walked to the TV section of the room.

He sat for an hour and a half, watching an action movie consisting of guns, sex, and the good guys winning at the end. Then, after his wait, he walked back to his car to use his AMT. He put in the memory and placed the device on his head.

Flick

The smell of still oak air fills the room as the black-haired woman walks into the church, hand-in-hand. The walls made of mismatched shades of gray bricks held the lighting from the colorful stained glass windows, piercing the sun like a sword sticking through the building. Her per-

fume smells of roses and cherries, as she sits near the back of the room on a long wooden bench. The minister stands behind the podium in a pure white cloak as he begins to speak.

"Love everyone!" he shouts as the small crowd cheers him on, and a feeling of happiness and unity falls like rain onto all those finding love.

"Amen!" a woman from behind shouts.

"Love everyone!" the nameless girl with black hair shouts.

"Fuck!" Madox shouted, throwing the AMT into the passenger seat as questions riddled his mind. His stomach twisted with happiness and confusion.

"Keep reality relative," he spoke to himself as anger injected itself into his stomach. "Well, what the fuck is reality?!"

He picked up his phone and dialed the memory police as tears ran from his eyes.

"Hello, what is your emergency?" a voice on the other side of the phone spoke.

Madox's mouth opened, but no words came out. The images of Denis, Joshua, and the girl from his memory riddled his mind. *Do I remember even though it hurts? Should I try to find out what's really going on?* Madox hung up the phone, beginning to bang on his dashboard.

"Fuck-fuck-fuck!" he shouted, not knowing what to do.

His childhood and memories told him to call the memory police, but his conscience fought against it for some unknown reason. Suddenly, he put his car in drive and took off. Quickly, he made it to 'A Drink to Remember' and walked inside with footsteps of anger. Finding Denis in his usual booth, he sat down next to him.

"We need to talk," Madox spoke, snapping to the bartender to get him a drink.

"Well, it's going fine, thanks," Denis said, staring at the wall, taking a drink of his beer.

"Can I ask you something? Something that could get you in trouble?" Madox did his best to talk quietly.

"Shoot," Denis seemed unfazed.

"How do you guys make memories?" he asked, as the bartender handed him his drink.

Denis put his drink down and looked over to Madox, "Why would you want to know that? You know me telling you could get both of us in serious trouble," he spoke in a grim tone.

"Well, I warned you," Madox took a swig of his drink.

Denis's eyes became like hawks as they shot through Madox.

Madox downed the rest of his beer, "Sorry, I fucked up. Now talk to me," he shot back in the same solemn tone.

Denis leaned back in his chair and chuckled, scouting out the room to make sure nobody could hear, "Fine by me... The process has a few different departments. We have the visual department that does the scenery and such, and the sound department that does voicing and whatever you hear. Then there's the feeling department, which I don't even know what they do there; all I know is they create the feeling in the memories. Then the last stage is to get it verified by the memory police; we have to send everything in to get checked by them. I'm a lead memory director, so my job is to be the center of all the departments and put the memory together. I get sent a memory I'm supposed to create, then a few writers and I, and set directors figure out how to make said memory. We have to write the lines, make sure the visuals are just how they want, and make sure to not violate any of the memory police guidelines. The easiest ones are informational memories; all we need to do for those is reuse the same asset of a man in a black suit, then overlay it with a voice line of whatever it needs to be. We actually reuse a lot more memories than people realize. However, some are complex with lots of tricky details. Like for a beach resort memory, we have to make sure they bring nothing back with them. No souvenirs or anything. Nothing to prove the memory was fake. That's why we send it to the memory police to get it checked. If they find anything that could compromise someone's personal reality, then it's a no-go. We do also use the fragility of memories to our advantage as well. Like if someone wants a memory with someone they know, but they don't want to go to the memory police, we just put in a filler character to which the user subconsciously fills with whoever they want. It's a bit more complex when you get into the small details, but that's overall how they're made," he said calmly, taking another drink of his beer.

"Do you ever make memories knowing they aren't true?" Madox said, snapping to the bartender for a second beer.

"You and me both know Mem-Co is what makes truth reality," he put down his drink and leaned in. "I don't know what's going on, but you talk like that, and you'll get yourself killed, or worse," He turned back facing the bar.

Madox stared into his second beer, looking straight down the glass as he spun the liquid at the bottom. His stomach felt empty, yet like it would explode. His mind tangled in itself as he thought of what he needed to do next.

The next Sunday quickly came, as Madox had been thinking about it all week. He and Kris decided on hall number three once again and watched football until it was time for service. Everyone got up to leave the auditorium, but Madox continued to sit in his chair while his fingers ran lines along the armrests and his foot tapped on the floor. Kris couldn't care less about Madox as long as she got her cassette, and swiftly left without him.

A few minutes rolled by, and suddenly a light flicked on behind the screen. Madox walked to the front of the auditorium, next to the hidden door. The same person as last time opened it, holding a joyful smile on his face after seeing Madox. The two walked down the rough, spider-web-filled hall and into the small room with the same few people sitting in their same seats as before.

"Madox! We're so glad you decided to come back!" Joshua greeted him warmly, patting the seat next to him.

"Yeah, I guess I just had to see what this 'true Christianity' really is," Madox said skeptically, taking a seat.

They all looked at one another again, with Joshua nodding to the man who had let Madox in. He took a deep breath while closing his eyes.

"I'm sorry for keeping it such a secret. It's just that there aren't many true Christians left in the world after Mem-Co. And it's hard to find people we can trust to tell this to," Joshua said in a meek tone.

"So then why me?" Madox asked.

"Because of this," Joshua said, pulling off his sock and shoe, revealing the words 'Madox Rightly' in faded ink. "I found this after the mission trip, and I know I wouldn't have risked writing it unless I found someone with a good heart who might take our message."

Madox could feel his skin crawl as he saw the word. Like a stalker writing, 'I love you' on his windshield before leaving for work. His stomach boiled in fear and anxiety, knowing that being here could get him in trouble with the memory police.

"Don't worry! It's okay! I promise!" Joshua tried to calm him down.

"So you saw how good I was on the mission trip and decided to tell me?" Madox asked in his same, held-back voice.

"You can say that," Joshua gave a tilted smile.

"Okay, so then, what is it? What is this true Christianity? I have my AMT in the car, you can just give me the cassette," Madox pushed, even more so intrigued to hear what he had to say.

He took another deep breath and closed his eyes, "No-no, you won't be needing your AMT. You see, true Christianity revolves around a person named Jesus who lived thousands of years ago. And what we believe is that He is the Son of God, who is the creator of the universe, and He came down from heaven to die for our sins so we can be in heaven with Him. And we get all of this from a book called the Bible," he said with a smile, pulling out a small wrinkled book with a leather cover, reading the title 'New Testament' in the front center, holding it out for Madox.

Like a rocketship, Madox could feel his stomach shoot to his throat. His brain shot flares of fear as the book sat in front of his face. Madox had never seen a book before, let alone heard of a 'God' or 'Jesus' character of any kind. He could feel himself tilt back in his chair as his face echoed in horror.

"I know-I know what you might be thinking, but please, please just trust us. We don't want to hurt you or get you in trouble in any way. We just wanted to tell you about Jesus and give you this. I marked a few spots in here for you to read. The only reason we are giving this to you is because Jesus tells us to love everyone and to help bring them to Him. Everything we know and believe is in this book. So if you read it and want to never come back, that's fine, but we meet here every week, and would love to have you," Joshua said as the group's collective smile forced itself on scared faces.

Madox grabbed the book as though it were an active bomb and held it in his hands, shaking in fear. He slowly put the book into his pocket and stood up, heading for the door. He quickly walked out as Joshua followed him closely. Then, just as he reached the door leading into the auditorium, Madox felt a hand grab his arm.

"Please, please... It doesn't matter if you believe us; just remember us. You never have to come back here, just remember the name Jesus..." he managed out through his high, shaky voice as tears welled in his eyes.

Madox's stomach flipped over again, unable to make a noise or sound. His arms fueled with adrenaline as he pulled away from Joshua and ran upstairs into the lobby. His heart pounded as his chest pumped like a hurricane. Questions rolled in his head like maggots on a corpse.

Tear Drop —
Sadness
Regret
Emotion
Having knowledge?
Love others?

"Here, I got you a cassette," Kris startled him, popping out from his side. She handed him a cassette as she began dragging him out the door.

He walked with her, trying to get as far away from the church as he could, as though a bomb was about to go off. They got in the car, and before Kris could even hand him the AMT, he had already made it out of the parking lot.

"Aren't you going to remember the sermon?" Kris asked, confused.

"Damn it!" Madox shouted. "I'm dropping you off at the house and going out."

Kris's face looked as though she had seen a body drop to the floor. The car filled with dead air, both knowing she wouldn't remember any of this ever happened. Madox dropped Kris at the house and sped back to the library.

On the drive over, his head filled with images and feelings colliding with one another. 'Ignorance is bliss', 'Relative reality', 'Don't choose sadness, choose Mem-Co!', his childhood screamed, telling him not to remember everything he had learned so he would feel better. The feelings and sounds of church service melted like gold in his brain as they collided with the images of Joshua's tears, begging him to remember. 'Love everyone,' fought what Denis had warned him about. He could feel his reality begin to blur as differing beliefs and feelings made no sense in his head.

He arrived at the library and grabbed the AMT Kris had left in the passenger seat. In step with his heartbeat, he slammed the car door shut and walked inside.

"Where is the 'J' section?" he asked as though his life depended on it, walking up to the same librarian as before.

She pointed to a section of shelves opposite the entry doors. Madox searched through the boxes, trying to find something that could explain reality to him. 'Jumping off an Airplane: Extreme Adrenaline!', 'Jeeps and Jets,' 'Join Mem-Co today!', he searched until finding what he was looking for. A box of cassettes, all labeled, 'Jesus' on the side.

He brought the cassette back to the librarian.

"That'll be one dollar and thirty-three cents, and it's twenty minutes," she told him, handing it back as he paid. "I don't know if you wanna do that one, though. I don't really know what or who Jesus is, but everyone who remembers always regrets it."

Madox looked at the cassette, wondering if whatever was on it would be worth remembering. Then the phrase he spoke wandered in his mind, 'Is bliss worth ignorance?' With a crooked face, he gripped his fist, knowing what he was going to do was against everything he knew. He marched into the back of the room and found a set of tables and chairs tucked into a corner, hidden by walls of cassettes. He sat down and peeked over his shoulder before slowly taking the book from his pocket.

Setting the book on the table, he scanned it as though it were a gun about to shoot him. His fingers danced along the edges, feeling the brittle pages and rough leather. He slowly opened the book, turning to a little sticky note stuck to one of the pages. The note read, 'John 3:16', where Madox quickly found it on the page.

"For God so loved the world, that he gave his only begotten Son, that whosoever believeth in him should not perish, but have everlasting life."

The words spoke like a bed of roses. Madox had no idea what to make of them. The phrase, 'everlasting life,' continued to ring like a bell the size of a building crashing on itself over and over. He flipped a few pages to find another note reading, 'Romans 5:8.'

"But God commendeth his love toward us, in that, while we were yet sinners, Christ died for us."

Curiosity overcame his fear as his eyes couldn't leave the pages. Like eating a mountain of sweets, his mind continued to fill.

Romans 8:38-39, "For I am persuaded, that neither death, nor life, nor angels, nor principalities, nor powers, nor things present, nor things to come, nor height, nor depth, nor any other creature, shall be able to separate us from the love of God, which is in Christ Jesus our Lord."

First John 4:16, "And we have known and believed the love that God hath to us. God is love; and he that dwelleth in love dwelleth in God, and God in him."

Revelations 1:8, "I am Alpha and Omega, the beginning and the ending, saith the Lord, which is, and which was, and which is to come, the Almighty."

Hours unraveled as his eyes scavenged the pages. The words of treason were so ripe with incomprehensible knowledge. Madox had no idea what most of the book meant, yet couldn't stop reading. Jesus rang in his head like a light filling in a void in his chest, he didn't even know was there.

Eventually, Madox's head grew too full of information he had to put the book down. He had never experienced anything so eye-opening yet impossible. He quickly put the book back in his pocket and walked over to the TVs in the center of the room, letting him cool off as questions rattled in his brain.

New Testament —
Scary
Is it truth?
Why not remember it?
Who is Jesus?
Salvation?

Half an hour passed in an instant as Madox held the cassette in his hands, reading the line 'Jesus' over and over. *What could possibly be on this cassette that's so bad if everything he had read described nothing but Jesus's love for people?* His curiosity crushed him as his fists clenched. He put the cassette in the AMT and put it on.

Flick

An empty room, with nothing but the faded whispers of wind and sunlight peering through the open window. A man with a genuine smile and long brown hair sits in a chair, making eye contact as the dark floor creeps on tearful knees.

"You are nothing. You will never be worthy. You are a sinner and will always be a sinner. You will die and be cast into fire and ash because that is all a sinner like you deserves. You are not loved, and will never be loved. Everything you do is wrong and sinful, you wicked person. Your life will be nothing but pain and anguish. Your teeth will grind as the snake bites your neck. Your skin will boil, and your eyes will tear. You deserve everything because of what you are and what you have done, sinner. Look to the sky and weep; nobody will save you. Fall to the ground, none will catch you. You have eaten the forbidden fruit and spat in my face, so you will die, you wicked sinner. And I, Jesus. I am hate."

Tears of red and blue fell like rain from Madox's eyes. His head burned as his grasp on reality melted into mixed shapes of emotions. Like two cars crashing head-on, the phrases 'I am hate' and 'For God so loved the world' tore apart Madox's head. With tears continuing to fall from his eyes, he packed up the AMT and shot out the door and into the parking lot. He threw open the door of his car and fell into the driver's seat, throwing the AMT in the passenger seat before slamming the door shut.

"What the fuck is Jesus!" he shouted, grabbing at his hair. In time, his blood cooled as his questions turned to exhaustion. He drove home, tapping his foot on the floor, trying to keep his thoughts out of his head.

"Ignorance is bliss," he spoke to himself, trying to calm himself.

Arriving home, he realized the only way to understand what was going on better would be to talk to Joshua back at church. He stuck the Bible under his bed like hiding evidence of a crime scene, and watched TV the rest of the night to block out his thoughts.

CHAPTER 7

The next day came, and Madox got ready for work as usual. He put on his clothes, made breakfast, and drove to work, anxious about what he could possibly do for a living. But more than that, he couldn't get the images of Joshua and Jesus out of his head. *Who is telling the truth? What is Christianity? Should I tell the memory police?*

"Good morning, Mr. Rightly! Mr. Dayfell is waiting in the lab department for you — just head down this hall and to the left!" Madox walked past the door greeter without saying a word.

The posters on the walls stared at him like eyes behind one-sided glass. 'Don't argue, just remember!' The phrases he had known since birth felt like weapons turned against him. *What if I don't want to remember something fake?* He thought to himself like a heart-attack waiting to happen. He walked into the lab, chattering with keyboards as a voice came from his side.

"Hey, Madox! Why do you look so grim today?" the man said, waving for Madox to follow him.

Madox followed quietly, staring at the floor. They made it through security, as Selleck introduced himself to Madox's unresponsive ears. Walking into the warehouse, Madox collapsed to the floor as tears fell from his face. Selleck gave him the cassette marked with 'For Madox' on the side.

Flick

Madox remembered everything and began arguing with Selleck before inevitably succumbing to his orders. Madox quietly returned to work, just like every other day. However, his head was louder than it had ever been before. It was as though this itself was proof that Christianity and Jesus weren't all they seemed. *What else is Mem-Co hiding? Why have they turned Christianity and Jesus into something they are not?* His head was filled with more questions than words on his clipboard.

He pushed through the entire day, fighting through the pain of knowledge. Finally, at the end of the day, he rushed to his car and began driving home. On his way, he saw a gas station on the side of the road, tightly swerving into the parking lot. He got out and rushed inside, grabbing the first cassette he could find. He rushed outside and into the car, placed the cassette into the AMT, and fitted it onto his head.

His finger sat shakily on the remote, unable to move as the images of the children slouched in their chairs roamed freely in his head. 'For God so loved the world,' rang through his ears as Joshua's tears fell like anvils on his chest.

"Fuck!" he shouted, tearing off the AMT and throwing it in the passenger seat. "Fuck-fuck-fuck-fuck-fuck-fuck-fuck!"

He put the car in reverse, heading home as his foot tapped furiously with his thoughts. *Ignorance is bliss, but is bliss worth ignorance?* Like a knife drawing blood, the thought tore through his mind as his conscience battled relentlessly.

Arriving at home, Madox rushed inside and into his room. Pulling the book from under his bed, he sat down to read, trying to make sense of who Jesus was and why Mem-Co would make him out to be the physical representation of hate. Hours flew by without movement. Questions piled higher with each turn of a page.

Suddenly, Madox threw the book against the wall with a shout, falling back on the bed with clenched fists. Both his knowledge and ignorance frustrated him profusely as he realized the only way to understand what was going on would be to talk to Joshua again on Sunday. After throwing his clothes off, he made his way to bed, fighting insomnia for an ounce of sleep.

The next morning, the sun rose with a wall of white clouds to cover it. Madox's alarm went off as he raised his head in the same position from when he went to sleep. Sluggishly, he slid out of bed, still wearing the same clothes. Walking to the living room, he patted his black shirt and pants to try and smooth them out, as well as straighten his black tie.

Static filled the air as the empty couch sat vacant in the middle of the room. He walked to the kitchen and made breakfast as he recovered from his doleful state of mind. He looked at his hand, holding the still black ink as though it showed the time and date of his death.

After eating breakfast, he walked to his car and began driving to work. Questions mixed with rage pressed on his chest, remembering all the things that had happened. *Christianity, Jesus, Joshua, what of all of that was real? Should I go back to Mem-Co? After everything they have done? But who will help the children? I can't just let those kids die.*

"Fuck me!"

Walking into Mem-Co, Madox's stomach grew into a boil of rage.

"Good morning, Mr. Rightly! Mr. Dayfell is waiting in the lab department for you, just head down this hall and to the left!" the woman at the front desk said politely, pointing down the hall.

"Fuck you," Madox responded without flinching, knocking the woman back in shock.

Down the hall, the signs stared at him, as though knowing what all Madox had done. Entering the lab department, Selleck stood in the middle of the room talking with a man in a lab coat.

"Madox, you're finally here! I'm Sel-"

"Shut the fuck up and let's go," Madox spoke without remorse, heading to the second set of doors. Selleck almost dropped dead as his dumbstruck face whipped around in confusion.

"You-you remember?" Selleck caught up as they reached the doors.

Madox gave no reply as his boiling stomach steamed from his face. Selleck realized the extent of Madox's anger and silently walked him through security and into the large child-filled room.

"Fuck Mem-Co," he whispered to himself before getting to work.

Hours stretched like walking through muddied water as Madox worked his usual routine. The images of the children's faces were imprinted on his mind as though he was plastering them like posters along the inside of his head. His stomach swirled in sorrow and hate as he tried to think of anything else to keep his mind off the poor children, but there was nothing. He had no way to know what memories were real and what were produced by the children drooling at his feet. Yet, everything he knew was real brought him nothing but pain.

Eventually, the end of his shift came, sending Madox to his car. His foot pounded the floor, screaming for him to turn into the gas station to take away his pain. Like an old film flipping through his mind, the images of the children continued to flash in his head. One after the next, their drool leaked faces, their numb bodies, the slight twitching in their thumbs after the flick of their headsets.

"I have to remember," he spoke to himself. "I have to remember them no matter how much it hurts."

Arriving at home, Madox stomped his way inside. After taking a shower, he went straight to bed. His eyes glared at the stars hidden behind the roof as he lay down, avoiding eye contact with the Veltik poster staring daggers into him. The film continued to roll nonstop, as though plastered right on the ceiling in front of his face. Hours vanished without a wink of sleep. He lay quietly, unable to move or speak as his brain continued uninterrupted until the sun greeted him warmly, like a warm, fluffy coat on a hot summer day.

The week drew out as the endless spiral of insanity bled into Madox's head.

Necktie — Lifeless Bodies — Wine Glass — Flickering Lights
Joshua crying, refusing to leave his dreams.
Necktie — Lifeless Bodies — Wine Glass — Flickering Lights
The book sitting like a bomb beneath his bed.
Necktie — Lifeless Bodies — Wine Glass — Flickering Lights
The futility of the mundane compared to the reality beyond reach.
Necktie — Lifeless Bodies — Wine Glass — Flickering Lights
Repeated arguments inside and outside work.

Necktie — Lifeless Bodies — Wine Glass — Flickering Lights
The poster of Veltik ready to kill.
Necktie — Lifeless Bodies — Wine Glass — Flickering Lights

Finally, Sunday had arrived. Madox shot out of bed, ready to find out what was going on. Dressing quickly, he put on his clothes and tied his black necktie. After Kris left the room, he took the book from under his bed and slid it into his pocket. The feeling of the book burned through his pants. On the drive over, Madox held a stone face.

"Is everything alright?" Kris asked, patting her face with makeup.

"Yes," Madox responded in a deep tone, sticking his foot to the floor.

"Alright," Kris responded, continuing to pat her face like a brand new paint job over an engineless car.

They arrived at church, hustling inside as Madox dragged Kris across the parking lot. Entering the building, Madox recommended hall three this week, but Kris refused and decided to go down hall one. Madox walked down hall three and sat down alone at the back of the theater.

Waiting in the large dark room, his eyes were unable to follow the TV. Images of Veltik flashed like red flags caught in a snowstorm. Questions piled in Madox's brain, ready to be thrown at a moment's notice. The book continued to burn through his pants as his conscience screamed to follow his gut, knowing the right thing to do.

The lights flicked on. Like cows to the slaughter, the entire audience rose in unison, piling through the exit doors. Madox froze in his seat as his mind darted around the room. His foot tapped wildly, dancing across the floor as though it was trying to scream for help.

With the last of the crowd exiting the auditorium, the lights flicked off. His foot came to a sudden halt as his eyes became glued to the blank screen. He waited a moment before shooting out of his seat, making his way to the hidden door in the side of the wall.

Walking down the aisle, each step crushed the ground, holding the weight of the book in his pants. He pushed open the door on the side of the wall before making his way down the dark web-filled hall. At the end of the hall, his head shook, finding an empty room with nothing but a few dusty chairs.

"They must be late," Madox whispered anxiously to himself before sitting in the seat next to where Joshua always sat.

Five minutes passed, no sign of anyone. Another ten minutes, and still nothing. *Where could they possibly be?* Madox questioned as his body could not contain his feelings much longer.

Another ten minutes, and Madox shot out of his seat. Back through the dark webbed hall, through the hidden door, and out of the auditorium, Madox sped with passion. Walking into the main room, Madox couldn't help but freeze in his tracks.

Dozens of bodies were sprawled half-naked on the floor, making love to one another. Each one of the people he had seen in the hidden room piled together, kissing and touching one another freely. Joshua sat in the middle, kissing a woman Madox had never seen before, while Kris made love to another man across the room. Madox could feel his fists grip in anger as his stomach churned in his gut.

"What the hell?" he whispered to himself, walking over to Joshua.

He carefully stepped over the bodies lying across the floor, grabbing Joshua by the shoulder and pulling him off the woman. Joshua seemed confused, looking up and down Madox.

"Love everyone! Did you want to join?" he asked, confused, sending Madox into even more of a rage.

"What, no! What are you doing? Can I talk to you in private for a second?" he asked, looking around the room to find he was causing a scene.

"Have we met?" he asked, looking around the room. His face held no recognition of Madox.

Like a bullet to the head, Madox felt his body go limp as his stomach sank to the floor. His eyes opened as wide as they could while his hands shook. The red swirling in his stomach turned to black as his chest lost all its air.

"No, no nevermind..." Madox let go of his shoulder and stood up, heading to the door.

They resumed what they were doing as though nothing had happened. He could see Danyella standing behind the front desk with a grin wider than he had ever seen, staring at Madox, causing the weight in his pocket to burn once again.

"You forgot your sermon, Madox," she smiled, holding out a cassette.

Madox froze right in front of the exit, while the door greeters stared at him like bodyguards.

"Yeah, I almost forgot," he walked over and grabbed the cassette, listening to the moaning of the bodies he had to walk over.

Just as Madox tried to grab the cassette, Danyella gripped it until their hands met in a stalemate.

"Love everyone," Danyella spoke softly, staring him in the eyes before letting go.

Madox could feel his heart pounding as he couldn't keep his hands from shaking. He began walking back to the exit before remembering Kris still making love to another man. His fists clenched once again as he walked over to her, tapping her on the shoulder. She looked up, disappointed, and sighed before slowly standing up and dressing in her clothes.

"Love everyone," the door greeters spoke as though placing guns to Madox's head.

They both walked outside and to the car. Madox sat down with a loud thud before starting the engine. Kris softly got in on the other side and shut the door before crawling to Madox, kissing him on the neck.

"Get off me!" Madox shouted, pushing Kris off.

Kris's face exploded in confusion and terror as she sat back in her seat.

"You expect me to let you do that after what I just saw you do with that other man?" he shouted at her.

"What does it matter what I was doing with him? Just don't remember it and you'll be fine! Ignorance is bliss," she shouted, grabbing the AMT out of the back seat and throwing it on Madox's lap. "I mean, the past few weeks you haven't exactly been performing for me, now have you!?"

Madox could feel his anger boiling in his throat as words of spite flew through his mind. He took a long sigh before putting the car in drive and setting course for home. Kris sat silently in the passenger seat, looking out the window, as Madox's face turned to stone. His foot tapped across the ground, trying to decipher the storm in his head.

"Ignorance is fucking bliss."

Arriving at home, they both rushed inside. Madox headed straight into his room while Kris headed straight for her pile of memories lying on the couch. In his room, he threw the book out of his pocket and began pacing back and forth.

Why did they get their minds erased? What is true Christianity? Does it have anything to do with Jesus, or is it just mindless sex and loving everyone? Why would they be so desperate to remember Jesus if he was so awful? Why would they risk having a book and telling people about Jesus, knowing they could lose everything because of it? If ignorance is bliss, why do people want to remember? Why can't our realities have Jesus in them? Why can't I just forgive Kris and choose not to remember it ever happened? Should I erase what happened? Is bliss worth ignorance?

Like sinking into an endless body of water, Madox choked on his own ignorance and knowledge. He gripped his face as his feet continued to pace around the room. His mind roamed freely as his emotions followed close behind.

Tears rolled down his cheeks as the realization that his questions would never be answered crushed him like a boulder. He sat on the bed and took a few long, deep breaths, trying to clear his mind from thought. He walked to his dresser and pulled it from the wall. Behind it, sat a white dusty air vent humming softly near the floor. He bent down and pulled the cover off. Reaching into the vent, he pulled out a black marker — the same one he used to write on his hand whenever the ink faded. He walked back over to the bed and sat down, staring intently at the marker.

"Memories," he whispered to himself. "We need memories to remember the important things in life."

He looked around the room until he eventually looked down at his body.

"Necktie."

He walked back over to the dresser, still pulled out from the wall, and wrote on the back.

Necktie —
A man going to work
A sign of respect
Treat me right
Don't ask about life
I just want to live

His hands shook as he continued to write. Wine Glass. New Testament. Dust Pan. Beer Bottle. Gas Station. Tear Drop. Dr. Veltik. Love Everyone. He could feel a smile grow on his face as though his inner thoughts and feelings rushed into the words. Even his fear subsided, as though somehow he could just drop it to the ground, never to be seen again.

Memories —
Are memories reality?
Is bliss worth ignorance?
What we are made of?
Who we are?
Can reality be relative?

CHAPTER 8

The scent of vanilla filled the restaurant as the lean table-top candle smoked softly between Kris and Madox, somehow managing to linger on without as much as a flicker of fire to keep it going. Deep red walls were lined with white Victorian swirls along the edges of the ceiling and floor. The floor formed a checkered pattern of white and brown tile. Dark oak tables were engraved beautifully along their seams.

Vivid blue and purple flowers sat in a clear vase in the center of the table, the candle smoking beside them. Madox wore a nice black tux with his usual black tie, while Kris wore a flowing aqua blue dress with white flowers sprinkled throughout. In front of them sat neatly folded napkins and untouched utensils, her wine glass already refilled four times. Couples sat around them, draped in silk clothes and warm smiles. Not a second passed without the distant laugh of a stranger.

Madox sat quietly, staring into his wine glass as his foot tapped across the floor. The two decided to go out for a nice romantic meal, celebrating Kris's solving of the murder of Mr. Dewpen. She deciphered the case right after church, ending with a craving for Ms. Moshly's food and wine after discovering the crab was only $29.99. Holding in her findings all day, her voice let loose like the opening of floodgates, explaining her brilliant solution to her most devious case yet. However, to Madox, her words felt more like distant echoes as he listened to the conversations of those around him.

"Oh, yes, and George, how is he doing?" a woman in a purple dress asked the woman sitting across from her.

"Who's George?" she asked, confused.

"I have no idea," the woman in purple replied as they both laughed and drank their wine.

"Mem-Co is such a wonderful company," a man in a tight black tux told the woman sitting in front of him.

"Mem-Co, it's where your dreams come true!" the woman replied just as Madox had seen and heard a thousand times.

"So what will you remember once we have our kid?" a woman asked the man sitting across from him.

"I'm thinking a sex yacht with all the most beautiful women on the planet for nine months, how about you?" he replied in a delighted voice.

"I'm going to explore all around Europe. Paris, Rome, London, Venice, and all over the place! I'm going to eat so much good food, meet so many people, and see all over this beautiful world," she replied just as cheerfully.

Madox's stomach churned. His foot sped along the hard tapestry-lined floor as questions rolled through his head. *How can all these people stand to act like this? Like zombies in a collective trance devised by Mem-Co.* The more he listened, the more similar their voices sounded, blending together like the static of a TV. *Is this how I've been acting my entire life? Just another cog in the machine produced by Mem-Co?* Vomit curled up his throat.

"Are you even listening?!" Kris hissed across the table, shooting Madox's head from staring at his glass.

"Yeah, yeah. Just keep talking..." he spat out in a flat voice.

"So yeah, as I was saying, after stopping by Ms. Moshly's food and wine and realizing the crab was only twenty-nine ninety-nine, I went back to the crime scene to check the air vents. And not to my surprise, I found the documents I needed to-"

"Do you ever feel bad using all these memories? It's like you don't even know who you are. Like you're not even a person, but just a collection of thoughts produced by Mem-Co. When was the last time we talked with each other about something that wasn't in the past? I don't live in the past. I want to talk about the present. The here and now. Like, who even are you? What are you thinking right now that isn't just some corporately made memory from the past?" Madox blurted out, unable to hold back.

Kris's face sank into a pale white, unable to talk or blink as she looked him in the eyes. The world around went silent as the air filled with tension.

"You're not a detective. You've never traveled the world or gone on a beautiful vacation in your life. Honestly, who even cares? It's not like you're even going to remember this conversation by tomorrow, so why am I bothering talking to you?" Madox watched as Kris's hands shook, knowing she was seconds from reaching for her phone.

A moment of silence passed as they both began to think of their next move, as if a flinch could detonate a bomb beneath their feet.

"So what can I get for you two tonight?" a peppy waitress in a white shirt over a red dress appeared next to them.

"Yeah, so I'll have the eight-ounce steak, medium rare, with a side of broccoli, please. And my wife would love the crab. She was informed they were twenty-nine ninety-nine while solving a murder mystery this afternoon. Oh, and do you, by chance, sell memories here? My wife seems to not be feeling well and would love to remember something other than that," Madox spoke softly, giving a warm smile to the waitress.

"Oh yes, of course! Give me just one second!" She ran off toward the kitchen and came back a moment later, holding an AMT and a cassette.

She handed Madox the cassette, giving the waitress the most genuine smile he could.

"Thank you!" he said softly.

"You're welcome!" she said in her same peppy tone, before walking back into the kitchen.

Madox's face dropped as he placed the cassette in the AMT. Then, setting the time from five minutes ago to present, Madox handed the cassette to Kris, still holding her same pale face. She snatched the cassette and pressed it to her head.

Flick

A tidal wave of color flowed back into her face. She took off the AMT with a loving smile.

"Oh, don't you just love Ms. Moshly's food and wine!? It's just the most wonderful place to be!" Her voice was filled with excitement.

Madox sighed before downing the rest of his wine, "Yes, it is a wonderful place. But you know what I've been thinking? I think you're the best detective I have ever met in my life! The way you solved the murder of Spline Gunter and Joules Rought, and now Mr. Dewpen? It's simply incredible! Do finish the rest of your story about how you solved the case," he said as he ground his teeth.

"Oh, yes, yes of course," she seemed confused yet excited, continuing from a little before where she had left off.

The night flew by like a bird without wings. Madox sat in his chair, listening to the many conversations around him, yet not the one he was in. The more he listened, the deeper his stomach sank, as though he was drowning in society itself.

Eventually, the waitress arrived with their food, yet even a full mouth didn't stop Kris from continuing to talk. Another half hour dragged on, and the torture was over. The two finished their meals and quickly headed out the door. Madox helped Kris walk to the car after having a few too many glasses of wine. She continued to stumble across the ground, talking and laughing about memories faded through her withered reality.

"Yeah, and you remember my day trip to Greece? Oh, it was so romantic, I wish you could have been there," she spiraled off. "Oh-oh-oh, and when I had sex with our neighbor Ralph, he was even better than you!" she laughed hysterically.

Rage boiled in Madox's stomach. He let go of her and took a step back.

"Ope," she giggled, hiding her mouth with her hand. "Whoops, I guess I let that one slip."

"Don't bother coming home," his voice shook in rage.

It was as though that single line sobered her immediately. "Wait, what? What are you talking about? I'm going home with you," she spoke, scared and confused.

"No. Don't come home," he spoke without remorse as the anger rose with his thoughts.

"You have to be joking! It was one time! Are you really going to let this one little thing ruin our marriage?! Just remember something else, I think we have a memory in the car you can-"

"Shut the fuck up!" he shouted, forcing her to take a step back in fear.

"I don't want any of those fucking memories! I want to remember! I want to know what you did, no matter how much it hurts me!" His words were knives.

"I-ignorance is bliss," she whispered as tears rolled down her cheeks.

"No, it's not. Ignorance is not bliss. All ignorance does is hide problems; it doesn't make them go away. I could choose not to remember all the awful things you've done, but that doesn't make them disappear! No matter what I remember, you still would have slept with him! And this cycle never ends. But not this time. I want to remember this so I can remember why I hate you."

Kris fell to her knees as tears streamed down her face. Madox walked the rest of the way to the car as Kris was too shocked to move. He opened the door, and just before getting in, he turned back to her.

"Call the memory police and tell them to erase any memories you have of me. I would say it was nice knowing you, but as of now, I never knew you."

Street lights rolled overhead, flashing beneath the charcoal sky. Madox leaned back on his seat, head against the headrest as his foot finally stilled. His mind felt numb as his hand gripped the steering wheel, going fifteen miles per hour over the speed limit on the open road. The distance between him and his house continued to grow as he continued to repeat what he had said in his mind.

"I want to remember this so I can remember why I hate you." his words sat in his stomach like a poet hanging by a noose.

Hours crept through the night as the car drove deeper into the dark abyss. Madox picked up his left hand and looked at it. 'Mem-Co 9AM-6PM' staring at him in ink that seemed to darken the farther out he drove. *I don't want to remember. I don't want the pain of knowledge.*

Walking into the house, the first thing Madox noticed was the empty couch. No wine glass or Mem-Caster in sight. The stagnant air filled the room as though he were dreaming. His stomach turned from anger to guilt, fully beginning to realize what he had done. *How many years did I throw away? How many memories of us together would be erased from Kris's head? All because I chose to remember.*

"No," he told himself, walking into the bedroom to escape the static of the couch. "I need to remember."

He threw himself on the bed, still wearing all his clothes. His body relaxed as his mind continued to roam. The dresser in his closet caught his eye, as if he had hidden a body inside. Hours ticked by until the clock on his side table displayed the time '1:34.' Madox let out a deep sigh and closed his eyes.

"You seem awfully quiet. I don't even think I've seen you blink once," Denis said, snapping his fingers in front of Madox to wake him up.

They sat at their usual booth, each holding a half-empty beer. Waitresses walked around in their skimpy outfits as brutish men cat-called them with bubbled voices. Madox faced his head to the table.

"Come on, talk to me, what's up?" Denis tried him again.

"How do you not remember something you want to remember?" Madox asked, looking up at Denis, taking another swig of his beer.

"I know if I were Mem-Co, I'd tell you anything that hurts you to know, you shouldn't try to remember. But for the rest of us who live in reality, well... Sucks to say reality is a painful place to live in."

"But what if it's something I want to remember but don't think I can live with knowing?"

"Man…" Denis studied him with a confused smile. "You sound just like you used to."

"What are you talking about?" Madox's eyes shot open.

"Never mind, I shouldn't have said anything," he leaned back in his chair with another swallow of his beer.

"Whoa, whoa, whoa-you can't just say something like that and not tell me more," Madox leaned in.

"Ignorance is bliss."

"Bullshit, what were you talking about?"

"Drop it. For both your safety and mine, I'm not telling you shit."

They locked eyes. The air thickened between them. Madox sat, leaning in, tapping the floor as his eyes shot daggers through Denis. Another swig from his beer, and Denis gave in.

"Jasmine," he said, folding his head back to finish his beer.

"Jasmine?"

"A girl with red hair. Find her, and she'll tell you more."

Madox's mind immediately flashed to the woman with red hair at the community meetings.

"Thank you," Madox said, leaning back in his chair.

"Don't get us killed."

Part Two

Empty, the seat next to Madox felt like the open wound of a scar attached to his body for years. The people around him smiled widely, filling the auditorium with fake memories bouncing along the walls. His foot tapped the ground, listening to the conversations of the people, thinking about what Denis had said.

"Oh, have you remembered the Puppy Playtime set? It's to die for!"

"Ms. Moshly's food and wine sounds amazing right now."

"How's your husband doing?"

"I don't have a husband."

"Of course, I just didn't remember."

"Ignorance is bliss!"

"I love Mem-Co! They are just the best!"

"Keep reality relative!"

"Hi'ya Madox! How's it goin'?"

Madox's head snapped toward the sound. Ralph and Julia Limon stood wide-eyed, waiting for a response. Madox felt his fists clench as his eyes stabbed through Ralph. Their smiles felt like fangs as their eyes seemed to glow red.

"You alright there, buddy? Where's Kris at?" Ralph asked politely.

"Get the fuck away from me," Madox said as his hands shook.

Their smiles dropped like bowling balls. They looked at one another and back at Madox in confusion and terror.

"Whoa-whoa there, I'm not sure what's causing all this, but I'm sure a quick memory could fix you right-"

"I said, get the fuck away from me!" Madox shouted as his legs shot up, and eyes across the room began to stare.

"I'm so sorry about him," he felt a soft hand on his shoulder as his vision blurred red. "He's having some stomach issues today, so it's best if you leave him alone."

Madox turned his head to find the woman with red hair standing behind him, smiling kindly with her beautiful face. The red haze faded to pink, and his hands lost their anger.

"Oh, of course," Julia said with a quick smile, as they both walked off, holding faces of disgust.

The lights dimmed, and Madox and the red-headed woman sat down, with her sitting in Kris's usual seat. Madox felt his chest press in and out as his foot tapped wildly on the floor.

"Watch the movie, I'll explain later," she whispered as the screen flicked on.

Light flashed from the screen as the movie played. Everyone watched silently, holding wide smiles on their empty faces. Madox's wide eyes stared forward, unable to take in the screen's colors. His mind flickered with questions of who the woman next to him was and what all she and

Denis knew. Not only that, but he knew what was coming after the film ended. He would have to fake remembering.

Yet, somehow Madox couldn't help but feel at ease around her, as though just her presence was able to calm him down. Even so, his mind knew nothing about her, raising more questions. *Why am I so comfortable around her for no reason? Is this another Mem-Co trick? Are they just testing to see if I need to be readjusted into society?*

An hour and a half of flickering lights, dull laughter, and sex scenes later, the screen went dark, and the lights turned back on. The people in black clothing began walking down the aisles, passing boxes of cassettes and AMTs down the rows. Reaching Madox, he took out his cassette and AMT and put it on, listening to the crowd.

"I love Mem-Co," the people spoke one by one.

"Take it, they will know," the red-headed woman said, fitting the AMT on her head.

"No, I don't want-"

"Do you want the memory police dragging you out of here? Take the memory," She spoke forcefully.

Flick

A light flash flicked from her eyes.

"I love Mem-Co," she spoke without hesitation.

Looking around the room, eyes of the people in black began to stare at him, as though they somehow knew he didn't want the memory. His mind flashed with images of the children and Joshua. The worlds behind his dresser ran through his mind.

"Shit," Madox said, placing the AMT on his head.

Flick

The beautiful, warm sun smiles happily along the shoreline. The sounds of waves and seagulls calmly playing overhead. A cute couple laughs wildly, splashing water on one another. The beaming cool glass of lemonade tastes so sweet as the condensation drips coolly down the edge into the soft, warm sand. The shady umbrella stands, stabbed into the sand, slightly tilted over the beautiful woman lying peacefully in nothing but a small blue bikini.

A handsome man with shiny bulk muscles, wearing nothing but a pair of blue swim shorts and a pair of shades. His head turns over as he begins to speak in his low, friendly tone.

"Isn't this wonderful?"

"Yes, it is."

"The warm sun, amazing food and drinks, and gorgeous people having endless fun. This is what I want the world to be. Luckily, because of Mem-Co, this is what the world can be, but it all starts with you. Anytime you hear or find something outside of your own reality, make sure to immediately report it to the memory police to ensure happiness for everyone. Any time you are feeling down or learn something that makes you upset, make sure to remember something else instead of that awful memory. Remember, ignorance is bliss and reality is relative," the man stood up, walking to the ocean. "Come with me. Let's have some fun on this amazing beach."

Laughter fills the air as the cool water shines in the sun. A game of volleyball is played in the water, while laughing women in bikinis and muscular men with veins popping beneath their skin talk with one another joyfully. The serene horizon turns into a gradient display of red and purple as the sun begins to set over the sea. The man in the blue swim trunks walks back over, holding a smile warmer than the sunset.

"My name is Dr. Veltik, and I am so glad I got to spend this time with you, all thanks to both you and Mem-Co. I love Mem-Co! Say it with me!"

"I love Mem-Co. Fuck!" Madox muttered through clenched teeth, throwing the AMT off his head.

"Cool it. Follow me out of here," the woman said as the crowd began to stand up to leave.

Filing through the crowded exit, a murder of crows circled overhead. Their wings flapped in the distance as they pecked through the herd of rotting sheep. Cawing screamed from a distance, as more continued to flutter in. Their heads turned back and forth while their black eyes remained still. Caw, another screamed as the two finally exited the building, leaving the circle of birds flying overhead.

Tightly gripping Madox's arm, she led him to her car. Each step seemed to twist his head as he looked over, seeing the woman with red hair instead of Kris. She held a kind, plastered smile as people continued to walk by. Madox couldn't help but keep his eyes on her more than on where he was walking.

"I'll explain everything later, just get in the car, and quit looking at me like I'm your pet doll or something," she said tightly, still holding her plastered smile.

Sitting in her short red Jaytime Visual Deluxe Experience — four hundred horsepower, great for special guests, priced at $300,000 — which Madox had ridden in only once before, his foot began tapping rapidly on the floor. Without saying a word, the woman put the car in drive and set off on the road.

"Where are you taking me?" Madox asked as each of his emotions stood in line to speak to her.

"Out to eat," she responded lightly.

"What? I thought you wanted to go somewhere private so we could talk."

"Oh, we will talk."

"Can we just talk now? Who are you? Why are you doing this? Did Denis tell you about me? What do you know about me?"

"Wow. Denis was right. You sound just like you used to," she couldn't help but smile as she took a quick glance at him.

"What does that mean!? What do you mean used to!? What do you know about me!?" Madox's anger took hold.

"You still like the tacos at, oh, what is it called... Terrific Tacos! Yeah, that's the name of the place!" she said excitedly.

Madox gave her a face of equal confusion and disgust, "What are you talking about? Why won't you just answer my questions?"

"Why can't you just shut up and enjoy riding in this expensive car with a beautiful woman who's taking you to get tacos? I'll answer all your questions once we get settled and start eating. I promise it's not that far."

Madox didn't know if he would strangle her or himself first.

"You do like the tacos from there still, right?"

"I don't think I've ever been there."

"Oh, then you're gonna thank me by the end of the night!" she said with a giggle. "And I'm Jasmine if you couldn't already tell."

Her smile relaxed into a look of comfort, as Madox's body sat tense in his seat, continuing to run his foot on the ground. His body leaned on the car door, trying to keep his distance as much as he could. His eyes watched outside as the trees and buildings flashed past. The sun hung half-cocked in the sky, keeping enough light to see, but not enough to be heard.

Two minutes passed before they arrived at a small building with a metal grooved roof and bright yellow lights pouring out of the large windows. She parked the car before the two walked inside, Jasmine holding Madox's hand tight. The atmosphere was full of red and green, with light trumpets playing overhead. Around half of the tables were full of people, happily talking and enjoying their food.

"Hi! Welcome to Terrific Tacos!" A man in a white shirt and black pants came up to them. "Would you like a booth or a table?"

"A booth, please!" Jasmine said, wrapping her arms around Madox as she nudged her head into his shoulder, holding a smile brighter than Kris had ever displayed the entire time they were together.

The man smiled as he began leading them to a small booth in the corner of the room, Jasmine tightly gripping Madox's arm the entire walk over. Reaching the table, Jasmine let go so they could sit down.

The waiter put down two menus. "What would you like to drink this evening?"

"I'll take a margarita, and he'll have a Buddy's Beer, please!" she said before Madox even had the chance to think. The waiter smiled as he began walking away.

"So, did you catch the latest football game? I could have sworn we weren't going to win, but some-"

"What is going on?" Madox blurted out.

"Whoa, no need to be rude, we'll get to all that. Let's just enjoy the time we have right now. I promise you're gonna-"

"Gonna what?! I don't want to enjoy the time we have; I don't even know who you are or how you know me. Start talking to me right now," he said harshly.

Jasmine's sunshine slowly quivered into the look of rain as she looked into Madox's face of fire. She sighed as she pulled a small, folded-up piece of paper out of her pocket and put it in the middle of the table.

"Take this, it'll take you where you need to go to get more answers. But please, they're only letting me have this night. Can we please just talk? Get to know one another? I haven't gotten to see you in so long." Tears rolled down her face as she wiped them with the napkins on the table.

"Here you are," The waiter popped in, laying both drinks in front of them. "You all ready to order?"

"Yes, I'll have the chicken and rice, and he'll have the carne asada tacos," she said quickly, forcing a smile on her face.

The man scribbled the order on a piece of paper before walking away with a smile. Jasmine looked back at Madox, trying her best to hold that same smile. Madox noticed his foot pace across the floor as he leaned in on the table. Questions rolled around his head as they fueled a fire burning in his stomach.

"Haven't seen me in so long? How did you know me? How long ago? Were we together once? Why wouldn't I remember? Why would you come back to me if I had no memory of you? Who's 'they'? How do you-"

"Alright-alright!" she shouted off, putting her hands up to get Madox to stop talking. "I'll tell you what I can. I can't say what we were, or who you were. I'm honestly not even supposed to be here. Mem-Co allowed me this one night to get to be with you, as long as I gave you this," she pointed at the paper still sitting in the middle of the table.

Madox picked up the piece of paper and unfolded it, revealing an address and a date.

1332 Ariel Dr, 8:00 PM, Oct 25

"What's this?" Madox asked, examining the paper.

"They told me to give you that, and to tell you to be at that address at that time, but that's all I know. I don't know what for or why, that's just what they told me to tell you," she said, taking a long drink out of her margarita.

Madox looked at the paper a while longer before shoving it in his pocket.

"Why can't you tell me anything?" he asked, looking into her eyes.

"Because of what we were. Because of who you are. Fuck, you really are just how you always were. So curious yet naive," she bit her lip as her eyes watered once again. "So, can we just talk? Please?"

Her finger tapped on her glass as she forced an almost loving smile on her face. Still, Madox couldn't see past the red boiling in his vision. Each unanswered question sat like a bomb waiting to go off. *How can I just talk when there is so much I need to know and figure out? Why did Mem-Co tell her to give me that paper? What is it for?*

"So, are you still into sports? If not, we can talk about something-"

"Just stop talking! I don't even know you, and you expect me to just talk with you? As far as I know, you could just be a part of the memory police, trying to see if I've gone off the deep end, right? Or some past experience I wanted to never remember, maybe there's a reason I don't remember who you are! Why should I listen to you? You're lucky I don't call the memory police right now!" His words cut her as tears rolled down her face.

Her hands shook as her lips quivered, "H-honey, I just-"

"Honey! Don't call me that! I don't know you! Why am I even here if you can't tell me anything?"

"P-please stop..." Her tears turned to rain, "I-I missed you. I haven't gotten to see you in so long, please just listen-"

"Here's your fo—"

"Shut up!" Madox snapped, standing up, as the waiter arrived with the food.

Jasmine was now fully sobbing in her seat as Madox stood angrily staring at her. The waiter's mouth hung open as the restaurant stood in awe.

"I don't know you, and if you won't help me, I don't care who the fuck you are," he shouted, storming out of the building.

Like an atom bomb crisping Madox from the inside out, his anger burned through his skin. His chest pumped as his fists gripped tightly. Then, realizing Jasmine was his ride, his voice screamed into the open air before beginning his walk back to the Community Center to get his car.

As he walked, his mind raced to and from the center, finishing hundreds of laps a second. He pulled the paper out of his pocket and looked at it. *What does it all mean?* Fortunately, on his walk over, he passed 'A Drink to Remember', and decided to go in to talk to Denis.

Walking inside, the atmosphere was the same as ever. Girls in skimpy outfits, constant laughing, and smiles. Even the smell of alcohol and cigarettes gave a comforting feeling. He walked to the back of the building, to their normal spot. Surprisingly, Denis wasn't there. Madox couldn't remember the last time Denis wasn't in his spot.

"Hey, you seen Denis?" Madox asked the bartender, turning his head to look around.

"Who?" The bartender seemed confused.

"Denis, the guy-" Madox paused, "uh-never mind, thanks."

Madox shot out the door, turning his hustle into a run. Luckily, the Community Center wasn't far. Madox got into his car and shot out of the empty parking lot. His foot pounced across the floor as the speedometer kept a constant speed of ten miles per hour over the speed limit.

Soon, he arrived at Denis's house and almost sprinted up the front door. The sun was now down as the moon began peeking overhead. Two black lamps lit the large, dark oak door with soft yellow lights. Lit windows surrounded the door, revealing the white interior of the house. Madox rang the doorbell three times and stood waiting with his foot lightly tapping the concrete ground. The shadow of a person walked up, before hearing a light click and the opening of the door.

"Oh, hi Madox, what can I do for you?" Denis's wife, Rachel, said politely as her face hunched in confusion.

"Is Denis home?" Madox shot at her.

Her face looked more confused. "Who?"

Madox's stomach sank to the floor as anger pierced through his eyes. He stomped his way back to his car without responding, speeding off to his house.

"Fuck-fuck-fuck!" He shouted, slamming his head on the dash-board, "What did you do, Denis? The fuck did you do?!"

Frost crept over the empty land as the moon sat still. Pine-scented air flowed softly past the frozen trees. Sounds of rubber pressing the ink bridge spanning between Madox's house and his thoughts.

Dim yellow lights rolling overhead like a shield from the untouched sea of white freckles. A hot glow radiates from the foot, pressing into the gas.

Silhouettes of stones carved into crosses. Scratches cover the un-known faces, unable to gnaw at the minds of their loved ones. Vultures circled overhead, pecking each other's wounds and revealing bones. Comforting black, the night resides endlessly, covering the grievous monsters. One lit match revealing endless sorrow. Light too bright yet dark too null.

Half a mile from his house, Madox continued to fume through the night. Then, a shot of panic rushed through his chest as the image of two black squares fell into his vision. Rolling up to his house, the two squares became cars parked in front of his house. Madox rolled into the parking lot, fighting the endless wave of thoughts shooting like knives through his stomach.

His body froze, the only sound coming from his foot tapping the floor. Images of Veltik telling him not to remember, mixed with the words of Denis, Joshua, and the children. His words repeated through his mind, 'Is bliss worth ignorance?' as the idea of recourse dissipated into the cold.

Shakily, Madox's hand opened the car door as his feet took him inside. In the living room stood three men in full padded black suits, covering their feet to face.

"Are you Madox Rightly?" One of the men asked as their expressionless masks tore through his chest.

"Yes," he responded softly.

"Your acquaintance, Denis Long, has been found unable to abide by Mem-Co policy. Mem-Co found fit to provide him with a better life, improving his personality to fit into society. We have been tasked with correcting reality so that Denis Long no longer exists. That includes all memories of him," the man in the middle pointed to the couch, "Have a seat, Mr. Rightly."

Vision fuzzy. Air heavy. Madox stood still. Escape would not only be difficult but pointless. If caught, they'd erase his entire life rather than just Denis, and if he somehow managed to escape, he would be on the run the rest of his life. His hands shook as his foot quivered on the floor.

"Five minutes," Madox said softly, surprising even himself, "Five minutes in my room to remember him. Then you can take it all."

Silence boiled like tar. All three stood lifeless, continuing to tear into Madox's chest.

"Two minutes. We will be posted outside the room," the man said lifelessly.

Weak-kneed, Madox walked over to his room, escorted by two of the men. He walked in, softly closing the door behind him. The room felt empty, where only Madox's screams of anger could fill the void. Yet the only friend to comfort him was the poster of Veltik stabbing Madox with anxiety and anger. Madox walked over to the poster, fists tightly gripped into his palms. With a sudden swipe, he tore the poster off the wall, throwing it on the floor.

Tears rolled down his face as reality crumbled around him. He quickly ran to his dresser and pulled it out from the wall. Taking the marker from out of the air vent, he began to write.

Red Hair —
Knows me
Useless
Liar
Can't remember
Is she real?

Death —
Death of body
Death of mind
Unable to escape
At least remember
Love is to remember

Bang! Bang! Bang!
"Time's up!" The voice shouted from behind the door.
Madox quickly turned from the dresser to the wall. As quickly as he could, he wrote two words in large letters, circling them multiple times.

Remember Denis!!!

Bang! Bang! Bang!
"I said, time's up!" The voice shouted twice as loudly.

Madox threw the marker into the vent and pushed the dresser back in. Tears of red and blue fell as he walked to the door, revealing him to a room void of color.

Sitting in the rectification center, gray beams shriveled through the bland windows. Colorless brick walls formed around the crowd, who were sitting in cold metal seats. Madox could feel his hands trembling, watching the man with a ball and chain walk into the neighboring room, escorted by men wearing black robes covering their heads to their feet. Blurred faces in dull suits stared through the glass, other than the image of a woman in red weeping in the corner. They all watched through the windows as the man took a seat in his wooden chair. Like a phantom, Madox felt the cool metal helmet pressing upon his head and the tight metal straps gripping him to the chair.

Madox's foot tapped along the ground, shooting like a gun through the empty tomb of air. His eyes were glued to the man's face, sitting frozen in his seat. A man in white walked into the neighboring room, walking up to the man before standing in front of him. Through the glass, the audience was unable to hear what was said. Only the man in white stared at the chained man, unfazed by his words.

Tapping furiously, Madox's foot tried to escape as the man in white walked to the back wall, holding a large metal lever. The air froze as the man reached his arm for the handle, preventing Madox from taking another breath. A loud clank flung through the window as the wisps of white flashed from the chained man's head. Watching in both terror and awe, the crowd stiffened in silence.

Pounding, Madox's heart raced as his foot froze under his breath. He watched the man's face in agony, slowly dimming into an unretained blur. Each second sped faster and faster, as his heart turned from terror into a numb blend of confusion and boredom. The woman in red's tears quickly faded as she watched the flashes of white fly from the blurred figure. The crowd soon questioned why they were there and began to walk out the black metal door.

"It's time to go," a man in black forced Madox to his feet, dragging him to the black door.

CHAPTER 9

1332 Ariel Dr, 8:00 PM, Oct 25

Madox held the paper Jasmine gave to him as he stood in the middle of a cracked pavement road, facing a large, rundown building. It was held together by nothing more than burnt wood blending into the black sky. He found himself in the middle of the woods. There were no other buildings nearby, and even the driveway was a three-minute drive from the main road.

He looked around. No other cars or people were in sight, making him question whether he was not only in the right place, but whether this event was even real. *Maybe a con artist trying to mess with my memories. Or a trap Mem-Co lured me into.*

"Mr. Rightly, right this way, sir," a voice came from the broken building.

Madox turned around and, to his surprise, found an older man in a perfect black tux standing in the middle of the rubble-filled building.

"Is this for the-"

"Yes, sir, the Mem-Co chairholders' banquet. I will take you right away if you would so kindly follow me," the man said, gesturing further into the debris with his pure white glove.

Mem-Co banquet? What could they want with me? Madox stared at him wide-eyed. Cautiously, Madox began walking into the burnt building, stepping over heaps of charred and splintered wood planks sticking from the floor. The man walked further into the rubble, leading him to a large opening surrounding a metal square. The man stepped onto the metal square and waved to Madox.

"Right here, sir." He gestured next to him.

Madox stood on top of the large metal square, with the suited man holding a formal smile on his face as he waited. The man lifted his right arm to his collar and pressed a tiny button, making a small beep.

"Do be careful while the elevator is moving," the man said as the floor slowly sank into the ground.

Madox's mind worked overtime as fear, anxiety, and curiosity bounced around his head like a bullet in a metal room. The images of the children at Mem-Co and Joshua's crying face flashed in his mind. *Would there be a group of memory police down there to trap him? Maybe something worse that I don't even know about.*

Around ten meters down the hole, the light from the moon cut off from a trap door above as a warm, glowing light peered through the widening gap in the wall. Eventually, the elevator lowered far enough for Madox to see what was happening.

A huge square room, thirty meters in every direction, was covered in red and gold patterned tapestries, with white pillars shooting from floor to ceiling. There were multiple glass chandeliers sparkling like diamonds, casting bright, shimmering light above the beautifully crafted mosaic spreading across the floor. Around thirty men and women were dressed in spotlessly tailored clothing, flashing billboard smiles at one another. They all talked and laughed softly, holding trembling glasses of liquid as waiters dashed around with trays of sparkling champagne. A table in the corner held piles of cake and sweets, along with a line of colorfully arranged cassettes.

Madox's eyes widened as his head began to fume.

"I think I'm not supposed to be here. Can you take me back up?" Madox turned to the man anxiously.

"On the contrary, you are the guest of honor, sir. Please make yourself comfortable." The man reached out his arm, gesturing to the party as his gentle smile sat calmly on his face.

Madox's head turned to the party, then back to the man, then to the party.

"Guest of honor?" he whispered to himself as he slowly stepped out of the elevator.

He spun around to the noise of a loud clank as the elevator rose back up into the ceiling. His heart pounded as the sounds of rich laughs and dinging glass grew louder in his ears.

"Champagne, sir?" Madox jumped as a waiter seemed to appear next to him out of nowhere.

"Oh—uh—no, no, thank you," Madox spat out.

The waiter dashed away without a word. Madox took a deep breath before walking slowly into the crowd. There were multiple smaller groups of people. A few people were talking one-on-one, some eating cake and using AMTs, while a large group near the center stood around talking. Madox walked into the large group and began listening to a woman in a bright, sparkly red dress howl joyfully.

"-and remember the one about the-the what was it?" she spat as her right hand began to snap. Her jumping left hand spilled champagne over the floor.

"Sex with an octopus!" a man shouted from the other side of the group as they all let out a loud roar of laughter.

"Yes-yes!" The first woman shouted through bright laughter, "People actually went out and bought memories of having sex with an octopus! Those people are crazy!" The group fell about, trying to contain their laughter.

"Wait-wait, Tiffany, you're pregnant!" The woman in the red dress pointed at another woman holding a nine-month bulge in her stomach while she downed what looked to be her fifth glass of champagne.

Her eyes doubled in size as she looked down with a mouth full of champagne, before spitting it out as the crowd boomed in laughter with more force than the first time.

"Oh my! I completely forgot! It must've been that 'Trip to Paris' memory that overwrote my memory of having this baby!" They all continued rolling over themselves in laughter.

Madox's face broke in terror as his stomach dropped to the floor. He slowly walked backward, still listening to their conversation.

"Do we still get memories if they're stillborn? I suppose it doesn't matter, I won't remember it anyway!" They fell about the place as Madox retreated to the cake table.

There was a cake of red and white spotted in pink roses, one blue and purple with hints of golden yellow accents, and a huge three-tier cake with golden ribbons and flowers spiraling around it. Next to them lay a row of colorfully assorted cassettes. Madox began running his fingers through them. 'Sex with Max Thump', 'Day spa for a year', 'Around the world and back'—just a few of the many titles Madox rolled his fingers through.

Then he picked one up, 'Beach House Fun: EXTREME.'

"Oh, good choice," a deep booming voice came from behind as Madox felt a thick hand on his shoulder.

He flipped around to find a large man in a dark gray tux. His face was rippled with fat, and a hotdog-sized cigar glowed in his mouth. He was bald and had eyes so covered in fat it was hard to believe he could see out of them.

"So glad you could join us for the party, Madox. It's been a long time since I've seen you," the man said, gripping hold of Madox's shoulder as he walked across the room.

"Who-who are you?" Madox spat out.

"Oh yes, of course—you need an introduction, don't you? Well, you can call me Dr. Veltik. We used to know each other very well in another life. Oh, and yes, I know you don't remember, but don't worry, the memory police can't get us down here. I was the one who invited you. I do hope you are enjoying the party," he boomed, pulling Madox around like a dog on a leash.

"Why-why did you invite me?" Madox managed out.

"Why? Well, you're the reason we are all here! You took Mem-Co from nothing and built it up to be the revolutionary corporation we know today," he raised his arms to all the surrounding features, as though it was all created by Madox himself.

"Because of me?" Madox could feel his stomach begin to burn as images of what Mem-Co had done to the world burned in his mind: the children treated like a computer, Joshua's crying, Kris half-dead on the couch, the woman drinking carelessly, not thinking of her child, even he himself was a symptom of Mem-Co.

"Well, yes, because of you!"

Saliva pouring out of a thirteen-year-old's limp mouth.

"You created world peace!"

Wine spilling onto the couch.

"You took away everyone's bad memories and realities and turned them into something beautiful!"

Taking people's lives with their memories.

"You have given the entire world something amazing..."

A void less, empty screen of flashing colors.

"Happiness!"

Madox could feel his blood boil as the thought of him creating a world like this poured gas on the fire in his head. He stared deep in Veltik's eyes as he raised his hands, about to start shouting, until he heard the clanging of metal on glass.

"Gather round, everyone," Veltik shouted, tapping his spoon and glass together, "Gather 'round!"

All the shareholders circled round them, sparkling cider and champagne in hand. Dr. Veltik raised his glass and looked around the room, "To Memory Corporation!"

The rest raised their glasses and cheered as though they had cured sin itself. Madox could feel his stomach continue to brew in rage as images fueled his mind.

"I'm glad you could all find the time to come to this wondrous meeting," Veltik began, "Because of all you hardworking people, this company has grown tremendously, and world peace comes closer every day! Not only that, but people are happier than they've ever been! Blissfully ignorant of whatever they want to ignore. But let us keep in our memory the one who truly revolutionized Mem-Co, with our special guest, Madox Rightly!" he shouted as the crowd cheered for Madox.

"No!" Madox broke out, unable to hold his anger pressing in his chest, "This is wrong! You can't just get rid of memories! Memory is part of being human! The good and bad work to develop character and individualism! Without memories, people have no personality, no humanity! It's like you're taking out their souls and replacing them with corporate slop!" he blurted out, leaving the room silent.

Veltik slowly walked up to him, standing in front of him with a half-cocked smile and ginger cider sparkling in his glass.

"Well, of course, we're making them corporate slop—that's the point!" he said ecstatically, "Not only can we control the people using our products, but they have no memory of it afterward! It's the perfect business! However, if you're looking at the moral implications of turning people into 'corporate slop,' just look at the numbers. Since Mem-Co started, the world has become better. Murder, rape, depression, and even war itself have plummeted to unknown levels. If people can't remember their own anger and sadness, then they won't hurt anyone. Not only have we helped society as a whole, but even in the individual, we have revolutionized instantaneous happiness! You find out your father died? Get rid of that old, awful memory and replace it with something beautiful! Find out your spouse has been cheating on you? Why destroy a perfect marriage when you can just erase it and live happily ever after? You see, we're not selling memories, we're selling ignorance. The world is a terrible place, but if you don't know how awful it is, then it can't hurt you."

"Well, the people still deserve the right to know about the world! To be humans who can learn and experience life outside of a cassette at a gas station!" Madox intervened.

"Ha!" Veltik blurted out, "Right to know? Learn? Experience!? Do you know about the world before we came along? Sure, they could sit down and read a book and retain the memory of what they learned, but is that what they did? No! They would sit in front of TVs and scroll on their endless phone screens for hours on end and not remember a single thing! They were corporate slop before this company was ever thought possible! They would choose to erase the horrors of this world before memory technology ever came to exist. There has never been individualism or learning in this world. Memories are a commodity humanity gave up years ago and replaced with instantaneous gratification. All we did was capitalize on the idea. And now people can remember their life as something amazing, with adventures and joy! Or would you prefer a world where people could have a full day off to 'experience' and 'learn' yet not be able to remember a single thing that happened? This corporation has expelled evil and sadness from this world at the cost of individual character, the world never really had."

"But that's just not true!" Madox objected. "People had beliefs, ideas, and thoughts of their own! They could think and act upon themselves based on their own memories and experiences, not just go off the corporate slop you addicted them to!"

"Ah, yes! And that leads to the reason for our celebration!" he cheered happily, turning around and raising his glass, "Here's to finally winning the war on religion!" They all cheered with him. Madox's heart sank to the floor so far that he thought he might fall to his knees.

"Wh-what do you mean you won the war against religion?" His voice trembled. "W-why would you—how could you?"

"Oh, so glad you asked!" Veltik said, like the popping of a cork out of a bottle of champagne, "Well, for the 'why' of your question, isn't it obvious? For peace, my dear Madox! How can you have peace while maintaining each individual's personal beliefs? That's a question we pondered for a while yet could never figure out, until we realized that's just plain impossible. Having Christians and atheists? Communists and capitalists? Nazis and Jews? They go together like fire and gasoline, literally in some cases. But there are a multitude of other people and beliefs that lead to nothing but conflict, and looking throughout history, we see that people choose to follow their own beliefs rather than find peace. As such, we realized that the only way to achieve true peace is to have the absence of beliefs. So, we got to work, taking out every belief from the minds of every individual. And thanks to our revolutionizing memory technology, we were able to do just that. At first, we realized taking out beliefs would be near impossible because we would have to take the memory of every single person who had ever heard of the belief. Take Christianity, for example, even if they aren't Christians, there are millions of others who have heard of Christianity. So, to get rid of the religion of Christianity as a whole would take replacing every person's memory who had ever heard of Christianity. So we took a more simple and clever approach, not only taking the belief out of Christianity, but replacing it with our own belief. We took the idea of being a Christian and reduced it to nothing more than being someone who 'loves people.' Being Muslim means 'loving nature' and let me tell you I am a huge atheist, if you define it as someone who 'loves science.' And it wasn't just for religion, but for every belief. Being racist means you 'get along with everyone,' and being a Nazi means 'valuing life.' So, regarding the war against religion, we won; we found 95% of people related to multiple religions, knowing nothing other than the memories we provided for them. You ask one hundred people what Christianity is, and ninety-five will say they love people. And for the five that do mention God or Jesus, we replace their memories, making it one hundred percent consistent. And sure, there will always be people who 'know the truth,' but what they don't realize is that we are what makes truth factual. They can preach on the streets and look like a madman before we replace their memories. And what has this done? What has getting rid of religion done for the world? It has eradicated conflict! No more wars in Israel or people getting killed overseas preaching to people who don't want to hear what they have to say. And this is true for all beliefs we have manipulated. It has resulted in nothing but peace, because without beliefs, nobody has anything to fight over. Our next victim we're thinking of will be marriage. Just think about it, you can't have a divorce rate if you don't have a marriage rate. No more fighting with your spouse or being bound by only one sexual partner. I hear you recently separated from your wife, if you even remember, but if you do, then I know you will understand.

Now for the 'how.' How would we pull off such an extreme scheme? Well, that's where you came in, Madox. You formed the perfect plan to get rid of belief. The first step was simple: get our products on every surface of every building across the world. Convenience stores, gas stations, hotels, and so much more. We had to fill the world with so much product that people couldn't help but taste the forbidden fruit shoved in their mouths. This then leads to the second step of your wondrous plan, getting people addicted to our product. This was tricky, seeing as it was more on the consumer than Mem-Co to get them addicted. However, with a product like ours, who couldn't get addicted to it? Books were one of the first things to go. Though it was obvious looking back, why would someone sit down and read for an hour rather than do something fun, then replace their memory with the content of the book? There was no more need to actually sit down and learn; just do whatever you want and still get the results afterwards. Libraries threw away books like they were infectious, but not only that, people soon realized they could create information through memories and use it for more than books, but normal day-to-day information. Why go to a three-hour-long meeting when you can work on mindless tasks for a few hours, then get your memories replaced with the information you need? Even Sunday services began handing out memory services for those who didn't want to attend church. And of course, this led to the third phase of the plan, where we really started warping memories to how we needed them. We began changing the knowledge in the memories to reflect the values of Mem-Co. Someone goes to the library to learn about God? 'A fictional character used to describe destruction,' I wrote that one myself. Go to Sunday school, and I bet all you'll hear is 'love others.' And that's what we want them to think. We want everyone to be good to one another, because our primary goal is and will always be peace. So then, in the fourth stage, we replaced the memories of anyone who still remembers. You start changing the definition of Christians, and people tend to notice, but if we completely switch their memories to one where they never heard of Christianity, then who's left to go against us? And rather than changing the memories of every single person, we just needed to go against the ones who stood against us, then the rest just fell into submission. At this point, we had everyone thinking, knowing, and acting how we wanted them to, but there was one big issue: reality. How can we have people believing and living their best lives when they have reality contradicting them? You find a Bible saying 'Jesus loves you' or a photo of a person in your wallet you tried to erase—that's when things start to get dicey. However, we learned quickly that people would much rather live in our fictitious memories than in reality. Why have beliefs or individualism when you can have happiness instead? As I said, people were trying to mimic a fraction of our greatness with TV and phones before we came along, blocking out whatever reality they had to find instant gratification in false ignorance. So, along with the problem of reality, we also had a second problem with the now mostly peaceful world not needing military or police any longer. And so came the MICP—how wonderful they are. They go and take any remnants of reality contrary to a person's memory and destroy it. And then for anyone else who still remembers the MICP, use the ML to replace that memory too. They even monitor TV and memories themselves to make sure they don't have anything that can contradict anyone's reality. How perfect is that? A world where reality can be whatever you want it to be? A world filled with sayings of peace and love, with nobody hurting one another? And the best part? We didn't have to hurt or kill a single person throughout the entire process! Every person is out there living their best lives, loving others, and doing well. Of course, we still have a ways to go to achieve perfect peace throughout the entire world, but we are making rapid progress each and every day. That is why we are here to celebrate our victorious war on religion, which couldn't have been done without your genius Madox, and that's why we brought you here. I was hoping you'd get off your high horse of morality and realize the good you've done. You created world peace! And for what? Senseless beliefs that created nothing but pain? You're the savior of the planet! In only a few years, the entire globe will be at perfect peace, all because of you! Everyone, let's give it up for Madox!"

The room cheered with whistles and light pats of hands as every eye faced Madox. They had open smiles like bloodied wolf fangs sticking into the necks of their sheep, which they call humanity. Madox turned to stone as the reality of who he was twisted his throat to where he couldn't breathe. More than that, he realized not only did these people know what they'd done to humanity, but they were ecstatic about it. *The deletion of beliefs from society as a whole?* He could feel vomit roll up his throat as they continued to clap and cheer.

"You're a hero!" the crowd shouted at him.

"You made all my dreams come true!"

"You've made me so rich and happy!"

He could feel his hands shaking as the crowd praised him like a god. *I can't even remember making this plan. Or my wife. Or this past life at all. And yet they call me the savior of the world? They say they have world peace when they overwrite the memory of their own loved ones as though they are something to be bought at a store and not cherished with love. Can there be connections in this world if nobody knows who anyone else is? Can there be love without connection? Can there be love and peace? Is the price we've paid for peace worth the expulsion of our humanity?*

Madox's mind revved like an engine spewing hot oil and liquid all over, melting his thoughts from the reality he thought was real. So many questions he didn't—couldn't—know the answers to, yet they were all caused by him.

"So, what do you say? Will you finally come join us and be a part of this wondrous world you've created?" Veltik asked, reaching out his hand with his same half-cocked smile.

Madox stood still, staring at the open hand in front of him as though he was signing a contract with the devil.

"No!" he shouted, smacking Veltik's hand away, "You-you people are monsters! You didn't save the world—you destroyed it!"

"Well, I'm sorry to hear that—I truly am…" he said genuinely, turning his head to the door, "Guards, would you please give our guest here a new home? And make sure it's a nice one. But leave no traces of Madox Rightly when you're done."

Suddenly, two arms wrapped around Madox as two men in full black gear pulled him off the floor. Madox began kicking and pulling, trying to escape, but it was no use. All the people watched silently as he fought for his life, knowing what they were going to do to him.

"Please! Please no! I need to remember what you've done! I need to remember who I am! I need to remember Christianity! I need to remember right from wrong! Please no!" he screamed as they dragged him out of the door.

Pulling him into a gray-tinted room, they shoved Madox onto the single metal chair sitting in the center. The door slammed shut as they strapped him to the seat. He closed his eyes as tears streamed down his face. Though they weren't killing him, they were killing the memory of him. They would go to every person who ever knew him and take away their memories. Madox Rightly would be dead and gone, even if his body remained alive. He would be like a true zombie, filled with nothing but false memories to give him the feeling of a happy life. His foot tapped the floor, screaming for help.

"Hey," a voice came from in front of him.

Madox opened his eyes to find a tall, skinny man with blond hair and scattered light freckles across his average white face. Holding a Buddy's Beer by the rim down by his waist, he stood staring at Madox. His face seemed tired, almost sad for what was about to happen. Madox looked around and saw that the room was empty except for him.

"My name is Denis. You and I used to know one another," the man said, taking a sip of his beer.

"What do you want?" Madox asked angrily through his tears.

"I want to talk—to explain everything," he said kindly.

"Explain what?"

"Who you were. What all happened to you."

"Why? I'm going to get my memories erased. Does it even matter?"

"No, I suppose it doesn't. But as I said, we used to know one another. Think of this more as a confession than a lecture. And I know you're curious to know about your past," he said, downing another drink. "Where to begin?"

CHAPTER 10

"Of course not! What are you thinking? Giving the public access to memory locators is a terrible idea. What do you think the entire point of this society is? It's to rewrite the past, making way for a more desirable present. Allowing people to look into the past would be our way of blowing society's own brains out," Madox said passionately, sitting in his wide, shiny leather chair while taking a long puff from his thick Cuban cigar.

"Well, what if people want to remember? How can we advance as a society without remembering anything? Someone could come up with the cure for cancer, then just erase it. How can we keep records of anything if the memory police destroy everything? There's no way society can function without some kind of written order or rule," Denis shot back, smiling as he leaned back in his tight leather office chair placed in front of Madox's three-meter-long dark oak desk.

"Everybody has memories they'd like to get rid of, even if they don't admit it. The ones who say, 'the past makes us who we are,' aren't wrong, but if you lose the memory of who you were, then there's no real loss, now, is there? That's what's so beautiful about our society: if something makes you unhappy, you can just get rid of it. Of course, most people think of smaller things like fights or something embarrassing they did, but let's think bigger. Imagine this scenario: You are a child, and you watch your father get drunk and beat your mother. Oh, and this isn't just a one-time thing. Almost every night, you find yourself hiding under your bed, plugging your ears. You hear the sound of the belt cracking on your mother's skin as she pleads for him to stop. *Whack, whack, whack...* Of course, there's nothing you can do about it.

You're just a small, helpless kid against a strong, grown man. All you can do is listen, already able to feel the leather belt cracking on your back, too. *Whack, whack, whack...* Eventually, one night comes when you're listening to the normal screaming of your mother until suddenly, it stops. *Whack, whack, whack...* You've always known how much you've hated listening to your own mother scream in pain, but you never realized how much worse it would be if she went silent."

"Okay—okay, I get it. You don't have to get so graphic. You're just saying we need to erase the kid's memories so he feels better. I get that," Denis interrupted, attempting to end Madox's story.

"Why, yes, that is one option. That's why we bring all the children to Mem-Co, ensuring no one has a traumatic experience when they are young, leading to more peaceful lives as adults. However, that was not where I was going with this story. Imagine, for hypothetical sake, of course, years later, after attending therapy and learning to re-integrate into society, you end up as a perfectly functional adult. Not only that, but you even learn how to be a better spouse from that traumatic experience. Most people would say this ending would be the best-case scenario, but I disagree. I think the best-case scenario is to erase the traumatic experience. You could argue that your past experience has helped you develop as a person, so why would you want to take away your character? My first counterpoint would be to tell you how little character you have in the first place. I mean, have you seen how some people act around restaurant waiters? Just awful. And I bet you've never seen as many middle fingers as when you're driving in tight traffic. And don't even get me started on the internet and social media. It's like a worldwide cesspool of babies. Oh! I heard the people from IT say they finished the beta for Mem-Book, so exciting! But anyway, as I was saying, nobody has character anymore. Everything is instant gratification, sunshine, and rainbows. So what does the little character you developed matter? My second counterpoint would be that even if you did get past your traumatic memories, that doesn't make them gone. The sound of your dad's belt, your mother's screaming, and her sudden silence, you can't take away. Even if you act all fine and dandy, you know, when you're alone in the shower, you can't help but sit on the ground and cry as the sounds ring in your ears like the screech of a fork on a plate. Luckily, I have the solution in a nice little cassette—only twenty dollars at your local grocery store. But of course, we've already established the problem isn't in losing the trauma itself, but the character developed from it. So why not remember? Choose not to remember your trauma or the character you developed. You won't even have the guilt of losing your character because you won't remember you had any to begin with! Now, you of course might ask, 'Then how do we give people character if you can't learn from your past experiences?' and the answer is right in front of you. We put the character into the memories we are replacing. Why have memories of your father beating your mother to help you become a better husband, when you could have memories of an amazing father and childhood, and wanting to grow up to be just like him? It ends with the same result, with far less trauma along the way. You could, of course, argue that the character developed from the trauma would be stronger than that of the false memories, but in a perfect world, what does it matter? Everyone will be happy and smiling anyway. What reason would there be to develop a character strong enough to require such awful memories? None, I'd say.

Then that leads into the second part of your argument: how could society advance without memories? First off, you choose what memories to keep, apart from the memory police, of course. If you learn the cure to cancer, then just remember it. It's that simple. Secondly, why would a perfect society need to advance? We can literally dissolve reality into whatever we want it to be, and you're saying there's going to be better? Who cares about the advancement of society! Just have fun! That's what we're all about at Mem-Co! Peace for everyone so they can enjoy life to its fullest! But of course, there are some operations where documentation is necessary to keep operations running smoothly. I would hate to be stuck in a hospital for months because the doctors aren't allowed to keep my documents. So we will keep some documentation alive, but we will keep it heavily censored and restricted. If a company needs some form of physical documentation, it will have to go through the memory police, who have every right to look through any documents they want at all times. But definitely nothing in our personal homes. No books, no writing utensils, no pictures or cameras, nothing that could compromise a person's own reality," he let out another puff of his cigar through his deep smile, drilled to his face.

"That's, well, brilliant. I never thought of it like that," Denis laughed as the gears in his head turned at full throttle, "Do you have any other topics you would like to discuss with me?"

"Not at the moment, I was wondering if you had any questions."

"I did think of one. You said they would just have to go to the store to replace their memory of when they were a child. However, without the ML's, how would they know when to replace their memory? I mean, it was years ago when he was a kid, would he have to erase his entire childhood just to get rid of those specific memories?"

"Of course not. Once again, that's what the memory police are for. They help to make your reality whatever you want it to be. If you want to erase your childhood trauma, just go to them, and they will make sure you have nothing left in your head that could make you frown! Though that does bring up a good point. We will probably need some location for people to do just that without them having to call the memory police every time. Luckily, I am one step ahead of the game. Mem-Co recently purchased a nearby cemetery, and as we won't be needing something that awful to remember our painful pasts, we are currently building our first of many Memory Halls on top of it. And as of now, it will be finished within the next three months," Madox smiled cheerfully.

Faint smoke from Madox's cigar floated softly through the dim air, illuminated by the only light beaming from the half-shut window blinds sitting on the wall behind Madox's chair. Opposite the window stood the only door leading in or out of the small, almost empty room, with nothing but Madox's chair, desk, and two guest chairs to fill in the empty space. The only item sitting on the desk was a half-full ashtray sitting in front of Madox, who was fitted in a deluxe black tux and nicely combed black hair. Denis wore a nice gray suit as he stroked his well-kept beard.

"Oh, look at the time! I'd best be off!" Madox shot out of his seat at the sight of his watch.

"Off to see her again?" Denis cracked, as Madox stamped out his cigar.

"You see right through me, don't you, Denis."

"Well, you've been seeing her a lot lately. Just last week, she even stopped by to bring you lunch.' But everyone in the office knows what was really going on. You two were in here for a while."

"Why do you think the desk is so cleared off?" Madox laughed as Denis threw a face of disgust.

"Anyway, hold down the fort for the rest of the day for me, alright. I promised her the rest of the day off because she has something important to tell me."

"Oh, any idea what it might be?"

"As long as it's not to break up, I couldn't care less," Madox laughed as he walked out the door.

Keyboards tapped, and phones rang all around the large but short room as people in fancy white shirts and black pants worked away. Papers lay freely over littered desks as loud, strict voices roamed the air. The smell of cigarettes and ink sat thick through the surrounding windows, letting in the bright yellow rays.

"Sir! A moment to talk!" Jace Veltik rushed over to Madox with a pile of papers in his hands, spilling a sip of his coffee over his shirt.

"I'm headed out, so be quick." Madox's stride spared no inch.

"Of course, sir! We've looked at the numbers, and there's just no way Congress is going to pass the memory police bill! We just don't have enough votes on our side. Apparently, they think Americans should have the right to their memories, and it's 'unethical' to take them away forcefully. Bastards don't realize the potential of the memory police! We could stop crime without having to kill or imprison anyone! I think they'd rather launch a missile than save a life just to prove their military budget isn't a waste," Veltik snarled in disapproval.

"Yeah, nothing we didn't expect. How about this, why don't you personally go to Congress and help them... Remember just how beneficial the memory police could be," Madox gave him a light nod before stopping at the front door.

"Oh, of course, sir!" Veltik grew a loud grin. "I won't let you down!"

Madox smiled before heading out the door. Outside, the trees swayed happily through the calm warmth of the sun. Flowers bloomed all around as the smell of spring danced sweetly through the breeze. Madox took a deep breath, filling his lungs with the lively air as he headed to his shiny black mustang.

Driving to the park, Madox couldn't help but smile in anticipation. His foot danced as questions ran through his head. *What does Jasmine have to tell me? Is it good? Is it bad?* He smiled wider, knowing that no matter what the news, he was just happy to spend time with her. Images of her wide smile and light red hair surfaced in his mind as his foot sped off even faster.

Arriving at the park, the parking lot was filled with about a dozen other cars, which was expected for such a beautiful day. The sky held a few large fluffy clouds in its cheerful blue air, while the sun sang its warm tune down to all the joyful people enjoying the park. A family at the park smiled as the mother pushed her daughter on the swing and the father played catch with his son. A young couple walked down the wide brick path, where not a single weed could break its spirit. Even an older woman was throwing popcorn to the ducks quacking gratefully in front of the small, round pond.

"Hey! Over here!" The sound of a bird's tweet rang through his ears.

Madox looked over to see Jasmine standing under a large, thick pine tree near the edge of the forest so others wouldn't bother them. She was wearing a wavy red shirt that sparkled in the sun, one Madox had never seen before. Next to her sat a small yellow blanket, holding a small woven basket on top as the tip of a wine glass poked its head out. Jasmine held her hair back as the wind blew, revealing her bright, big smile, which Madox had been waiting to see. They both walked to one another, meeting in the middle with a deep, long hug, followed by a quick, playful kiss.

"Why hello, my beautiful woman, you seem to have quite the setup here for the two of us. I hope I'm not dying," Madox joked.

"Yeah, sorry if this was too much. I just wanted it to be special when I told you," she bit her lip nervously.

"Well, you got me here, so what is it you wanted to tell me?" Madox asked, still holding her by the waist.

"Wait, tell me about your day first," she giggled as they sat on the blanket.

"Oh, just the usual. The app we've been working on should be out here soon, so that's a plus. But we're still working to get Congress to pass the bill we put through. Denis and me just finished talking about memory locators, but that's all just a bunch of stuff you'd get bored with. How was your day?" Madox changed the subject as the question of what she would tell him crept down his spine.

"I hope the bill passes, and I'll definitely have to try this new app when it comes out. But I haven't really done much today. I've really just been waiting to tell you. Ah! I just can't take it anymore!" She did a light scream as her body shook.

She took out two wine glasses from the basket and handed one to Madox before taking out the wine and pouring them both a glass. Their eyes glued to one another, as cheerful giggles couldn't help but make them both more excited. After pouring the wine, Jasmine reached into the basket for one last item. A small white object with a small blue piece at the end. She handed it over to Madox, who looked at it, realizing exactly what it was.

Madox dropped the object to the ground, revealing the two bright pink lines on the side, as he gave Jasmine a long kiss. They both laughed as they clinked their glasses to one another.

"This is crazy! We're going to be parents! I'm so excited!" Madox lay back on the blanket, "Wait, you shouldn't be drinking," his face dropped in fear.

"No, it's okay! It's not wine, it's grape juice I put in a wine glass to make it more fancy," she laughed as she took a small sip of her glass.

"Oh, you about gave me a heart attack." Madox's face drew back its color.

"I'm sorry! I'm glad you are excited, though! I didn't know how you'd take it exactly, so that's kinda why we're out here," she continued to giggle.

"I am so excited! How long have you known?" he asked with sparks flying from his eyes.

"Just a few days. I had been feeling weird, so I decided to get a test, and now I'm gonna be a mom!" she shouted, clapping her hands uncontrollably.

They both put down their glasses as they hugged and kissed one another, unable to control themselves in their excitement. Around half an hour went by, and they found themselves lying peacefully beneath the swaying trees, protecting them from the sun.

"What should we name them?" Jasmine asked.

"Well, I've always liked the name Madox the unstoppable," Madox laughed.

"You're stupid. I think Jen would be a cute name for a girl, what about a boy's name?"

"What about Max? I think that would be cute."

"That would be adorable!" Jasmine giggled as her hands fluttered uncontrollably, "Our little Max."

"No matter what, I know I'm going to love them so much! We are going to be amazing parents!" Madox shouted in excitement.

"Yeah, we are!" Jasmine shouted with equal energy before kissing once more.

Weeks flew by as every free hour of the day turned into baby preparation time. Both Madox and Jasmine found themselves reading parenting books and scrolling endlessly online to find the best cradle befitting their bee-themed room. The two had emptied out Madox's old office, which he never used, and painted the walls a bright, warm yellow. Somehow, they managed to have just about everything set up for the baby's new room, seven months before it was due. Still, they had much more preparing to do. They needed the baby's clothes, diapers, toys, food, and to baby-proof the entire house. Luckily, Jasmine prepared a five-page, detailed list of everything they still needed.

Around five months before the baby was to arrive, the two joined a parenting class to help prepare, as 'books can only do so much,' Jasmine liked to say. Madox was reluctant about the idea at first, as he had been missing work quite frequently already, but over time came to realize the baby was worth the time. They had to meet both Tuesdays and Thursdays at two, the normal time Madox would be meeting with Veltik to discuss politics. 'You can handle it,' Madox responded to Veltik's argument as to why the company needed him at such a crucial time.

By two months from the due date, the two had everything prepared. The room, clothes, toys, diapers, books, and everything else they could think of were all taken care of, apart from the classes they continued to attend. Jasmine now had a bulging belly, growing larger with her increasing excitement. Almost every night, the two would stay up late, talking into the night about their soon-to-be child and all the wild adventures they would have. If it were a girl, Jasmine would take her to dance lessons. If it were a boy, she would make both him and Madox do chores around the house for her. Madox had no preference for the gender, as long as they could share their thoughts with one another.

With the blink of an eye, another month flew by, and Madox found himself back in his office talking with Denis.

"Okay, let me try you with this question," Denis leaned in on his chair with a wide grin on his face, "How can reality be relative? I mean, just because I remember the sky to be green, that doesn't mean when I walk outside and look up, I'm going to see a green sky. Relative reality doesn't make sense in a definite world."

"Oh, yes, a good question indeed," Madox began as he leaned back in his chair, "Let me ask you: Imagine a pack of wolves finding a small helpless kitten on a road somewhere. The wolves then decide that instead of eating it, they will take it and raise it as their own. The cat then grows up with wolves and begins to act like a wolf more than a cat. It howls at the moon, does its best to hunt with the pack, and lives exactly like a wolf, believing itself to be a wolf. Does that make it a wolf?"

"Of course not, just because it acts like a wolf doesn't make it a wolf. Even the size comparison alone is enough for anyone to know it's not a wolf. And that works the same way with relative reality, just because the only memories the cat has are of wolves doesn't change the reality of itself. Memories can't alter physical space."

"Yet, we have a cat that will howl at the moon. Have you ever seen one do that?"

"No, I have not."

"Precisely! It doesn't matter if the cat is a wolf or not; all that matters is that it believes it is. Just like with relative reality, it doesn't matter how fake or true a person's reality is, as long as they believe it to be true."

"Well, then, how do we get them to believe their reality to be true? It's hard to believe the sky is green when you're looking at a blue sky."

"There are two things we need to do. First, tell them whatever they find in their head is the absolute truth. This is easy enough, as most people already perceive their memory to be reality. I can't blame them, memories are what we use to understand reality, a record of how the world works, we keep in this 'trusty' little safe of ours. If people were to go around and tell others their memories are fake, they wouldn't like that at all. For instance, your wedding, Denis. It was a great time, and I know we both enjoyed it. We both made fond memories there. What if I came up to you and told you those memories were false? You wouldn't like that. It doesn't even matter if the memories are false or not; all that matters is the feelings you get from the memories. You are very fond of the memories of your wedding, real or not, making you not want to lose them or believe they are fake. As such, people will choose to believe their memories are true, even if they are not, because the idea that they are false is worse than the actuality of whether they are or not. However, it does get difficult to convince some people that their memories are true when they know their memories can be altered. Yet, this is also another easy hurdle to overcome, as all we have to do is make them enjoy their memories. It's a lot easier to convince someone that a fun and happy memory is true rather than something sad or depressing. People want to perceive reality to be good and enjoyable, even if it's not true. So really, for the first step, all we have to do is sit back and say 'yes, you are right' and they'll all just believe us because that's what they want to hear. They say the sky is green, we tell them it's like grass on an open field. Then, when we keep agreeing with them, eventually they will look to the sky and tell creation it's wrong.

The second step to allow for relative reality is to make them want Mem-Co's reality. Yes, you could make the sky green, but why would you? Blue is such an amazing color for the sky. It's a reflection of the ocean, so any time you look up, it's like you're on the warm sunny beaches of Hawaii. Remember, we have control over the memories, so we can make them think whatever we want. If we want them to howl at the moon, all we need to do is fill their head with so many memories of howling at the moon that they can't help but get on all fours when it's peeking through the clouds. That's what's so amazing about this world! Because of this, we can truly make reality whatever we want it to be! If a man wants to be a woman, if someone wants to make their spouse disappear, if you want to be a wolf living in the woods, you can be!"

"But still, that's not reality. Just like the cat, even if you act like a wolf, that doesn't make you a wolf," Denis stepped in.

"Correct, but it doesn't matter as long as they believe reality is what they want it to be. You must remember, we make reality."

Denis laughed, admiring Madox's argument, "I see you haven't gone rusty after missing so much work the past few months."

"Well, once you know how the system works, it's quite easy to defend it," Madox smiled.

"Speaking of, how are you and Jasmine doing? How much longer until the baby arrives?"

"It's going great. We have the baby's room set up and all its clothing and other necessities picked out. Jasmine will keep going to work for the next few weeks, but we are just waiting for it to arrive. We still have a few more weeks of classes and have to see the doctor, but man, we are so ready for this baby! And it's only one month away!" Madox couldn't contain his excitement.

"And what did you say the gender is again?"

"We chose to keep it a surprise; we thought it would be more exciting that way."

"Whatever floats your boat, I suppose. You have names picked out yet?"

"Jen, if it's a girl, and Max if it's a boy."

"That's cute," Denis sighed, "I'll be honest, though, I never really found you as much of a kid person. I'm surprised with how excited you are."

"To be honest, I never really wanted kids, but for some reason, when I found out, I was just so happy. I don't know if it's because Jasmine was so excited or what, but now every time I think of having my own kid, it just makes me so happy. It's hard to describe."

"I'm happy for you, man. I hope everything goes just how you want it. I will say, though, Veltik is starting to get pretty upset with how much you've been gone lately." Denis shifted to a more serious tone.

"Who cares about what he thinks? Everything is running smoothly without me here to baby everyone all the time; he can take care of himself. I'm having an actual baby, and I'm not going to let work get in the way of it," Madox said lightheartedly.

Knock! Knock! Knock!

"Speak of the devil..." Madox said as Veltik swung open the door.

"You have a second to chat? We have a lot that needs discussing." Veltik said in a sour tone.

"Of course, what were you wanting to discuss?" Madox said calmly as Veltik closed the door and took a seat next to Denis.

"What are we going to do about the lawsuits against us? We have the entire U.S. Congress riding up our asses, and we're just sitting here twiddling our thumbs!"

"Lawsuits? Since when?" Madox asked, confused.

"We have hundreds of people claiming that we've infringed on their rights by changing their memories without their permission. Not only that, but they are claiming electoral fraud by manipulating Congress to vote in our favor. All of which you would have known if you hadn't been off playing daddy for the past eight months!" Veltik's ears steamed.

Madox could feel his blood begin to boil as his foot tapped on the ground. He closed his eyes and took a deep breath.

"First off, what grounds do they have to accuse us of this? I know we haven't given any ML's to find if their memories are fraudulent or not. They have no way of proving their memories are false. And even if they are, that doesn't take away their freedom to vote. They still have their autonomy to act how they wish, and if they remember something that makes them choose to vote a certain way, that's their own choice. Second, we have the ability to change reality to whatever we want. We just need to help everyone to remember what reality is. It doesn't matter how long it takes, but if we help every person in Congress to remember how amazing Mem-Co is, then there will be nobody to stop us. Third, don't talk to me about my family like that again," Madox spoke sharply.

A deadly thread of tension tore between Madox and Veltik's eyes as they cut one another with their gaze. Silence overtook the room as the temperature rose from all the boiling blood.

"Alright, let's settle down," Denis put himself between the two bulls.

"Madox wants time to prepare for his kid, but that is taking away from the time Veltik has to talk with him. So, how about we try to find a middle ground? Maybe you can go to class on Tuesdays, but have your normal meetings with Veltik on Thursdays?"

A moment passed, and the air filled with cutting silence.

"And I want you to stay late on Wednesdays to figure out these damn lawsuits," Veltik broke the silence.

"Why can't you do that? Isn't that what I pay you for?"

"You pay me to advocate in favor of Mem-Co, but if I don't understand how this company works, then it's much more difficult to argue a case for it. You know the ins and outs of this company, you hold its goals and morals. I need to understand why this company does what it does, and you are the person to talk to for that," Veltik slid his tongue.

Madox tapped his foot as his fists gripped together. His eyes turned to Denis, who gave him a light nod to agree with Veltik.

"Fine, Wednesdays and Thursdays only," Madox gave in with a fizzled sigh.

Veltik's face grew an unwelcoming smile as he stood from his chair.

"See you tomorrow," he spoke in his sly voice as he slid out the door.

"Don't let him get under your skin, I mean, you're as ready as you can be for this baby. Missing a few hours won't hurt."

Madox pulled a cigar from his desk drawer and leaned back in his chair, "I suppose you're right. Doesn't make Veltik any less of a dick though."

"Yeah," Denis let off a light chuckle before his face fell to the floor, "Though, this does bring up something I was wondering about..."

"Yeah, what is it?"

"It's just, you're so excited, yet, for the past few years, you've been preaching how Mem-Co taking everyone's children is what's best for society. If we keep going at the rate we are, Mem-Co will take your kid before you ever have the chance to be a dad. How can you be okay with that?"

Madox paused for a moment as his eyes stared at his desk.

"Honestly, that's a question I've pondered for a while now, and to be perfectly blunt, I don't have a straight answer. Logically, it wouldn't matter if the kid was taken or not, as long as I had new memories to replace them. If Jasmine and I are happy, then what would it matter if we had a baby or not? So logically, yes, I am okay with it. But then when I'm with her, I see how happy she is when she's talking about the kid and I just..." He took a deep sigh. "I just can't help but think maybe there are some things in this world worth being unhappy for."

"Almost makes you wonder if this new world is all it's cracked up to be."

"Yeah, really makes you think." Madox took one last pull from his cigar, sending the smoke from his mouth floating lightly across the room.

Around two weeks from the expected due date, Madox and Jasmine found themselves at home watching TV in their living room. They had a beautiful home with white quartz pillars and blemish-free chandeliers hanging overhead in almost every room of their twenty-six-room mansion. They lived deep in the woods, away from any building or person to cause them any stress.

Two small headphones attached to long wires came from Jasmine's large belly. A faint tune of classical music played from them. Jasmine lay upright on the couch, while Madox sat quietly in the single recliner.

Suddenly, Jasmine let out a loud whine as she grabbed her stomach, squeezing her face in pain.

Madox shot up, "What's wrong? What do you need?"

"It's nothing, just the baby. These contractions are getting worse," her face released its tension as she let out a defeated sigh, "I do have to go to the bathroom though."

Helping her off the couch, Madox slowly walked her over to the bathroom. Around halfway through the walk, Jasmine stopped suddenly as her eyes exploded. She gripped Madox's arm as her body shook.

"My water just broke," she spoke, terrified.

"What?! You aren't due for another-"

"Get me to a hospital!"

Madox helped Jasmine walk to the car and sat her inside as she gripped her stomach in pain.

"The baby is coming!" she wailed.

Madox had had much time to prepare and learn for this exact scenario, yet somehow the entire past nine months of his life seemed to fade from his memory as the adrenaline of the moment overtook his body. He threw the car in gear as he sped to the hospital. Jasmine squeezed his arm as his foot danced on the floorboard.

"Breathe in and out, in and out," Madox told her in hopes of calming her down.

Luckily, the two were not far from the hospital, and with the adrenaline-fueled speeding of Madox's car, they made it in a tight ten minutes. Flying into the parking lot and screeching to a halt in front of the main doors, Madox helped Jasmine up the stairs and inside. Opening the door, they were revealed to a tightly packed room of dozens of people, sitting and standing all around.

"Help! My wife is giving birth!" Madox shouted to the nurse who was talking with a grim-looking patient.

She quickly realized what was happening and shot into action. Within seconds, Jasmine was on a rolling bed, headed straight for the delivery room. Hooking her into all kinds of machines, Madox stood by her side as she squeezed his arm. Appearing in the room out of nowhere, the doctor began instructing Jasmine, telling her when to breathe and to push. Madox stood in a mixture of terror and thrill as the entire hospital seemed to dance around them.

Around an hour passed, and Jasmine was near the end of her torture. Waiting in intoxicating anticipation, Madox couldn't help but grit his teeth as his foot danced along the ground. He had been practicing the cutting of the umbilical cord for months, waiting for the day to finally arrive. His chest pounded in relentless anxiousness as Jasmine continued to squeeze and scream in pain.

Suddenly, the screams stopped as Jasmine's hand opened up. It was done, the baby was out. But like the shadow of a demon creeping over the newfound parents' shoulders, the most terrifying thing they could hear ripped from their ears. Silence. Like the memory of a blurred nightmare, unable to move or speak, no sound or thought, only fear rippling through their blood.

The doctors rushed the infant to the other side of the room, talking and yelling to one another. Madox's legs collapsed under the weight of his fear, and his body fell to the floor, landing on his rear. Unintelligible echoes flew in every direction as the sounds of the doctors grew louder.

"Where's my baby?" Jasmine cried as tears rolled from her eyes, "What's wrong with my baby? Is it okay? Tell me it's going to be alright! I want my baby!"

Madox couldn't move or stand. His body felt numb as his breath scratched down his throat. *Is it a boy or a girl?* Madox thought to himself. *Why is this happening to us? What did we do wrong? Please, please don't let this be real. I want my child. I want to be a father.*

Jasmine bawled louder as her cries produced no answer.

"I want my baby!"

CHAPTER 11

Beep-Beep-Beep-Beep...

Begrudgingly, Madox sat up out of bed as the alcohol-infused stench greeted him like a crow picking at his bones. Empty bottles of whisky, along with dirty clothes and other trash, were spilled around his room. Rubbing his eyes, he slapped the end table until he eventually turned off his screaming alarm. His eyes turned to the empty bed next to him, unveiling a long sigh from his chest.

Standing up in the drowsy darkness of the morning, Madox began dressing for work. Walking into the living room, he found the lights and TV still on, blasting their bright rays of light and sound across the spoiled room. Jasmine lay spiraled across the couch, clinging to an empty bottle of whisky in her limp hand. An empty box of tissues sat on the coffee table, with its contents scattered across the floor, filled with dried tears. Vomit spilled across the carpet as its stench mixed with the alcohol in the air.

Slowly and quietly, Madox cleaned the vomit off the floor and took the whisky bottle from her hand. After turning off the lights and TV, he carefully took Jasmine back to their room, tucking her in before laying a soft kiss on her forehead. Silently leaving the room, he quickly grabbed a bagel and some iced coffee from the fridge and headed for work.

Arriving at work, Madox headed inside, eating his breakfast along the way.

"Good morning, Mr. Rightly!" Debra, the receptionist, welcomed Madox, who gave a stretched smile and continued walking to his office.

On his way to his office, Madox spotted Denis sitting at his desk.

"Hey, you have a sec to talk?" Madox asked after walking over.

"Yeah, of course." Denis shot from his desk as the two walked to Madox's office.

"What's the matter? How are you guys doing?" Denis asked worriedly.

"I'll tell you when we're in my office," Madox responded before walking the rest of the way in silence.

"It's Jasmine, I just don't know what to do about her. She hasn't left the house in weeks. She drinks every night until she passes out. She hasn't been going to work. I'm scared she's going to do something drastic," Madox said worriedly, as Denis shut the door behind them.

Madox sat in his seat, resting his elbow on the desk for his hand to hold up his forehead.

"I know this probably isn't what you want to hear, but why don't you just take away your memory of the kid? This is exactly what you've been talking about. You could get rid of your pain and sadness in an instant and have nothing to feel bad about afterwards. If you're that worried about Jasmine, then don't let her remember," Denis said, sitting in his normal seat.

"We made a promise to one another that we would remember, even if it hurts," Madox spoke softly.

"Well, you could erase your promise, too. There's no shame in something you can't remember," Denis spoke in an equal tone.

Madox sighed before taking a cigar from his desk drawer. "Where did this silver tongue of yours come from?"

"I learned from the best," Denis leaned in, pulling a lighter from his jacket.

Madox took a long pull from his cigar, blowing it across the static room. Denis leaned back in his chair with an uneasy look on his face.

"How are you doing? You haven't been taking it the best either, you know. You've been staying late every night at work, drinking more than usual, and I can't remember the last time we met to argue with one another. If you need some time off, there's no shame—"

"No, I need work. It's how I keep my mind off things," Madox stepped in, taking another pull of his cigar.

Silence screamed over the dream-like air as Madox stared into his cigar with hollow eyes. His foot froze to the wooden floor. Denis couldn't lift his head, unable to convince himself of the reality he found himself in. The stagnant light piercing through the blinds covered nothing but the large desk, holding both Madox and Denis bound to the shadows.

"Well," Denis broke the silence after a few minutes, standing from his chair, "If you need to talk or need anything from me, just give me a call, alright…"

Madox responded in silence, as the soft shutting of the door came to close the rest of the day. Returning home from work around 8:30, Madox pulled into the driveway, dragging along static air through the night sky. Parking in the garage, he found himself frozen, taking in the dark, cool air. A deep breath rolled out of his chest as the faint light of the moon glared through the garage door window.

Walking inside, Madox prepared himself for anything he might find: empty bottles of wine, the stench of vomit and alcohol, the love of his life dangling over her thread of living. Yet surprisingly, there was nothing to be found. Madox couldn't believe how nice and well-kept everything looked. No empty bottles or tissues on the floor, no vomit or alcohol staining the furniture or flooring, and even the aroma of the room smelled of low-hanging apples on a tree.

"Honey, is that you?" A familiar voice came from the kitchen. "Dinner will be ready in a second!"

Tears rolled down Madox's face as he rushed into the kitchen to see his beautiful wife smiling vividly in front of him. She wore a fancy blue dress with nice black heels, standing next to the stove as the smell of sautéed onions and peppers came from the crackling pan. Madox rushed over, wrapping his arms around her.

"Whoa there, I'm happy to see you too," she said happily. "But you have to let me finish the food, or it's going to burn."

Madox took a step back, admiring her up and down with eyes of disbelief.

"I just thought it would be fun to dress up for you tonight, is that alright?" she said in a shy manner as her cheeks glowed red.

"Yes, of course, that's alright." He wiped the tears from his eyes. "Are you alright? You're sure you're feeling better?"

"Of course! Why wouldn't I be?" she smiled as she stirred the food.

Madox's stomach sank to the floor as his voice became empty. *Did she go to Mem-Co? Did she give in? That would explain why she's so happy all of a sudden. I don't see how else she could have recovered so quickly. But can I blame her? She's so happy this way. Fuck. I can't ever tell her about it. Fuck, Jasmine.*

"No reason. I'll go get ready for dinner," Madox said, clenching his fists and walking out of the kitchen.

Slowly, Madox took off his work clothes and ran a quick shower, putting on a nice shirt and pants for dinner after. Walking out of their bedroom, Madox found all the lights off except two dim flickering lights in the living room. Walking over, Jasmine sat delightfully at a beautiful candle-lit dinner. Red flowers and fancy dishes held delectable food spread across the table as Jasmine's shy cheeks blushed lightly.

"Sorry if this is too much." She bit her lip in a cute but shy manner.

"It's wonderful," Madox said, sitting at the table.

They both ate as the melting flames of the candles flickered across their walls and faces.

"So what do you think? Is it good?" Jasmine asked anxiously.

"It's amazing," Madox smiled lightly.

"That's good…" Her voice dimmed for a second as she took a drink from her glass of wine. "I'm sorry I sprung all this on you like this. I just wanted to say sorry for how I've been acting lately. I did my best to clean everything up, but I know I've been acting crazy, and I've made you deal with it, but you shouldn't have to. You are the most amazing husband I could ever ask for, and I love you. I don't know what got into me to make me do all that. I just hope you can forgive me."

Madox's foot crushed into the ground as his fists clenched each other tightly. He could feel himself shake as tears formed in his eyelids.

"You are the most amazing wife I could ask for. You have nothing to be sorry for," Madox held back his tears.

Is this the society I've created? Is this what I've done to humanity? What's the point of happiness if you can't remember those you love? I made reality so fluid that everything lost its meaning. Fuck me.

"I love you." Jasmine hugged Madox without him noticing her getting up from her seat.

"I love you too," Madox responded as happily as he could.

A few weeks flew by as Jasmine began living her best life. She started back up at work, quit drinking, and never mentioned their child. She had no tears or bad feelings coming from that awful memory, as though the baby itself faded from existence, living only in Madox's head.

Bang! Bang! Bang! The door to Madox's office knocked with the force of a bull.

"Madox, let me in! I know you're hurting, but you can't just lock yourself in your office and expect your problems to go away!" Denis shouted from outside. "Veltik has been talking to the shareholders about removing you from your position. Let me in to help figure this out with you."

Madox sat quietly in his chair. Biting silence overwhelmed his unstoppable thoughts. His hand moved under his desk, opening the bottom drawer. Reaching in, he pulled out a small silver revolver. Shaking, Madox's hands opened the gun to find a single bullet singing to him like the beauty of a sunrise. Quiet, peaceful, untouched by pain or sin. Pure bliss all at his fingertips. A stronger deterrent to painful memories than Mem-Co itself.

"Madox, let me in! I'm worried about you!" Denis continued to bang on the door.

Tears fell from Madox's eyes as thoughts of Jasmine and their child mixed with the reality of what he had created melted into his skin. Shutting the gun, Madox pulled back the hammer with his twitching hand.

His foot fought along the ground, begging for its life as it tapped away. Slowly, Madox raised the gun, placing the barrel on the side of his head.

Bash! Denis busted the door down.

"Fuck me, Madox, what are you doing?!"

Denis rushed to Madox, pulling the gun out of his hand. Tears gushed from Madox's eyes, seeing Denis's face filled with terror.

"What the fuck are you doing! Fuck me, Madox, you need help! We can help you! Please let me help you!" Denis pleaded as his eyes watered, pacing around the room.

"What do you want me to do? Live in my own happy little fantasy of a world?! When reality can be anything, then everything is meaningless! Even if I did pull the trigger, what would it matter?! You, Jasmine, everyone in the office could just take the memory of me out of their head without a lick of guilt, as though I had never existed in the first place! So what the fuck is the point of living if I may as well have never existed?" Madox shouted as tears continued to gush from his eyes.

"Because we want to remember you." Tears rolled down Denis's face. "Fuck, Madox! Memories are supposed to help people! Please let us help you!"

Silence broke as their thoughts began to squirm in a pool of emotion. Eventually, their final tears rolled down their faces as Madox's hands rested. Madox stood from his chair and took his jacket off the coat rack, heading for the door.

"Where are you going?" Denis grabbed onto Madox's arm.

"I have to get out of here. I want nothing to do with this place," Madox responded coldly.

Denis's face changed from anger to fear to worry as his hand gripped Madox's skin. Suddenly, Denis threw Madox's arm out of his hand in a wave of disgust.

"Fine, do whatever you want," he spoke angrily.

Madox stood for a moment before silently leaving the room. Walking through the office, Madox couldn't help but feel every eye dangling crooked looks over his shoulder. The signs hanging along the walls burned through his stomach, screaming their propaganda into his brain.

Don't choose sadness, choose Mem-Co!

Steam rolled through his body, boiling his blood.

Ignorance is bliss!

Fists formed in his hands as his body shook.

Keep your Reality Relative!

Sitting in his car, he slammed the door shut.

Memories are Reality!

"FUCK!" Madox screamed as he began banging on the dashboard of his car. As though something inside him had popped, all the anger built in his stomach steamed its way out. Suddenly, his hand moved to the transmission as he put the car in drive, heading for home. *I'm going to tell her everything. I'm going to tell her about our child. Our promise. I don't care if it hurts her. I'd rather she be sad than some corporate brain-dead robot under a facade of memories.*

One foot held his speed at twenty miles per hour over the speed limit while the other tapped along the floorboard. Steam continued to roll from his ears as he pulled into his driveway, the dark woods screaming around him. Slamming the door of his car, he rushed inside.

"Jasmine!" he shouted angrily, receiving no reply.

"Jasmine!" he shouted once again, beginning to look around the house for her.

Opening the door to the kitchen, a whiplash of emotion sank his stomach to the floor. Jasmine lay motionless on the floor, an empty bottle of pills next to her. Madox rushed over, tapping her face, begging for her to wake up. No response. Grabbing the phone out of his pocket as tears rolled from his eyes, Madox called 911.

"Nine-one-one, what is your emergency?" a woman's voice rang from the phone.

"M-my wife. She took too many pills. I need an ambulance," Madox fought through his tears.

"What is your location?"

"1332 Ariel Drive. Please be quick!" Madox begged.

"Unfortunately, our ambulances are all busy. It may take over a half-hour to-"

"What the fuck do you mean busy?! My wife needs medical attention now!" Madox screamed.

"We are having a surge in medical emergencies at the moment. I suggest that if you have the ability, you should take her to the hospital yourself. If not, we will be there as soon as-" Madox hung up the phone as he let out a deep scream.

Fueled by anger and fear, Madox threw Jasmine over his shoulder and into his car. His foot screamed with the scratching of the car tires against the ground, leaving skid marks in his driveway. Jasmine sagged lifelessly in the passenger seat as Madox watched the black road race behind him.

"It's gonna be okay," Madox squeezed Jasmine's hand lightly.

Reaching the hospital, Madox parked right in front, racing to pull Jasmine from her seat. Rushing inside while carrying Jasmine over his shoulder, Madox shouted for help. The room was filled with just as many, if not more, people than when Jasmine was in labor. A nurse noticed what was happening and quickly called for help. A team of nurses rushed into the room with an empty bed, speeding Jasmine into the emergency room.

Hunched over with his elbows on his knees, holding up his forehead with his clenched hands, Madox sat outside Jasmine's room. Doctors and nurses danced around like chickens with their heads cut off, pushing black body bags around as though the Grim Reaper himself was present. A clock ticked on the wall at a quarter of the speed at which his foot tapped along the ground. Racing like an endless wave of the ocean, crashing down on himself, Madox's thoughts poured tears through his stained eyes.

"Fuck!" Madox couldn't contain his emotions.

"Hey, what's happening?" A familiar voice sang in his ears.

Denis came walking down the hall, concern trickling down his face. Madox stood up and wrapped his arms around him as tears gushed from his eyes.

"I'm sorry," Madox spoke softly.

"It's alright, it's alright. I'll always be here for you. How's she doing?" Denis asked as Madox let go.

"They haven't told me anything. She's just been lying in that room," Madox responded as they both sat down.

"She's going to be alright, Madox," Denis tried to comfort him.

"What if it's my fault? I should have seen the signs, right? I just don't understand why she would do it if she had no memory of it," Madox fought with himself.

"No, it's not your fault. It's nobody's fault. Nobody could have known she would do this."

"I should have known."

Silence broke between them, other than the constant noise of the hospital around them. A nurse rushed by with another body bag as Madox clenched his fists in both fear and anger. The clock continued to tick as though counting down the last moments of Jasmine's life.

"Mr. Rightly?" A nurse walked up to him speedily.

"Yes! How is she? Will she be okay?" Madox's heart seemed to stop.

"Fortunately, yes, she will be fine. But she will need to stay here for the next few days. You're lucky you got here in time," she spoke words of relief through his body.

"Yeah, no thanks to your ambulances. I had to drive her here myself. What the hell is happening? Why are there so many people being rolled out in body bags?"

"It's that damned Mem-Co," the woman said angrily as Madox's stomach sank into the floor. "Apparently, they are telling everyone reality can be whatever they want, and to get rid of all the memories they don't like. Unfortunately, it seems people don't like to think about the concept of death. We have people left and right overdosing and jumping off buildings because they don't understand the consequences of doing so. To them, there's no need to be safe, because what's there to be safe from? This pill makes me feel good, so why don't I keep taking them? It's much faster to get to my car from my twenty-story apartment window than to go down the elevator. Oh heck, we had one man stab himself in the chest just to see what it would feel like."

Madox's legs crumbled under his feet, landing back in his chair. His mouth sagged open as his mind spat out nothing but an empty stare. Denis sat in the same bewildered manner, unable to move or speak.

"I have to go. You can stay here as long as you want and are free to see her if you wish," the nurse said, walking away.

The walls crept in as the sounds of the hospital ran with the passing of bodies. Vomit curled up Madox's throat as confusion and anger boiled in his stomach.

"What have we done?" Madox spoke shakily. "We have to put an end to this."

"End to what? Mem-Co? How do you expect to do that?" Denis snapped back.

"I don't know, but it has to end. I didn't realize all the pain I would cause. I was trying to help everyone, but only ended up damning them all."

Grinding his teeth, Madox couldn't help but stare at the floor as thoughts clogged his mind. Denis looked at Madox, realizing the pain he was in. He took a deep breath before placing his hand on Madox's back.

"Well, there's nothing we can do now. Let's get you home, alright. You need sleep. You've been through a lot lately," Denis spoke empathetically.

"No, I want to stay with Jasmine," Madox fought back.

"Madox, I'm your friend, and I mean this in the most loving way I can, but you look like shit and need to go home and get some rest."

Somehow, Denis's words made Madox realize how exhausted he truly was. His arms, legs, and head all seemed to sway back and forth, as though they had moments before falling to the ground. His eyelids felt like weights as his breath strained in his chest.

"You're right. Sorry, I'm such a dick. Let me just check on her before I go," Madox said softly.

Denis nodded quietly, sending Madox into Jasmine's room. Walking inside, the empty black of the night blew its way in through the open window. A cool breeze brushed along the pale curtains as the noise of the outside seemed to disappear. The only light in the room sat softly over Jasmine, her body resting peacefully under white covers. Softly, Madox walked over to the side of the bed, allowing him to see her beautiful face.

The heart monitor beeped as tears rolled from his eyes. His body crouched to the ground until his knees hit the floor. He took her hand and pressed it against his face, kissing and weeping. His cries bled into the night, begging to re-live the choices he had made. Yet, the night's only response came from the cool breeze cutting down his spine.

"I'm so sorry," he spoke softly through his tears. "I'm so sorry for everything. Please forgive me. I love you."

CHAPTER 12

Thundering into the building, Madox charged through Mem-Co with fire in his eyes.

"Good morning, M—"

"Shut up, Debra," Madox cut her off, turning left toward the lab department.

The signs on the walls felt like ghosts, screaming for him to turn back as his feet crushed the ground beneath him. Swinging the doors open to the lab, the sounds of hundreds of chattering fingers filled the large, packed room. Burning with a flame in his eyes, Madox walked to the center of the room, pushing over one of the workers typing at his computer.

"What the hell? What are you doing?" the man snapped.

Not listening, Madox climbed on top of the table, standing overhead for all to see and hear him.

"Listen!" Madox shouted, silencing the chattering keyboards in an instant as all eyes turned to him. "This is wrong! All of this is wrong! Memories aren't something to be taken out and manufactured! Take it from me! I know how much memories can hurt the ones you love. My wife almost killed herself because of these memories! Is that the kind of world you want to create? We need all our memories—the good and the bad—to allow us to grow as people instead of living in a false reality. And not only that, but memories are connections to the people we love! Even memories that make you want to throw the world away help you realize how wonderful good memories are. Without our memories, we take away our connections to others. We take away the importance of living! You might think you're creating a world of love and peace, but all you're doing is putting a mask over reality to make it seem better than what it truly is!"

"Well, maybe living in a good fake reality is better than living in a terrible real one."

The doors leading into the hallway burst open as Veltik and eight large men in black clothing walked into the room. Fear dipped into Madox's stomach as his foot tapped against the desk. He could see Veltik holding an AMT, knowing exactly what was about to happen.

"Take him down from there," Veltik said apathetically, pointing at Madox. "Sorry about this, everyone! It seems Madox here has finally gone off the deep end. Fortunately, I've been preparing for this very scenario."

"No! You can't take me! Veltik, listen to me—we have to put an end to this! It isn't right!" Madox fought as the men grabbed at his legs.

"Madox, you poor fool. I would have thought you'd know by now the true scope of memory technology. As you know, the morality of right and wrong is modeled in one's memories. So all we have to do to make things right is shape everyone's memory so they see Mem-Co as a savior rather than an oppressor."

The men finally grabbed Madox by his legs and pulled him off the table, sending keyboards and monitors crashing to the floor with him. Gripping his arms as they pulled him up, Veltik stood right in front of his face.

"Right now, you see Mem-Co as an oppressor. But we can change that with one little memory." Veltik shook a cassette in front of Madox's face.

Madox pushed and pulled, trying to escape the men's grasp, but there was no use. They began dragging him down the hall, through the entry doors, until they set him right outside the building.

"I will say, we haven't done an entire memory transfer on anyone yet, so this is more or less a trial run for us. But don't worry—we'll keep a close eye on you," Veltik said buoyantly as he put the cassette into a Mem-Caster.

"You won't get away with this. Someday everyone will see how awful Mem-Co truly is," Madox said, tears running down his face as Veltik placed the Mem-Caster on his head.

"Then we'll replace them all."

Flick

Silence.

For a moment, the world seemed to stop.

The tears in Madox's eyes turned to confusion. One of the men removed the Mem-Caster from his head as he looked around, bewildered.

"Hey there, Madox. How do you feel?" Veltik asked kindly.

Madox paused before responding. "Mr. Veltik, sir... what's happening? Who are these men, and why are they holding me?"

Veltik waved off the men, letting Madox go. "We were just helping you feel better with a new memory. Don't you feel better, Madox?"

Madox felt around his body, looking for any sign to tell him otherwise. "Yeah—yeah, I do feel better, Mr. Veltik, sir! Thanks for helping me feel better!" Madox shouted joyfully as he wrapped Veltik in a hug.

"Of course. That's what Mem-Co is here for—to make everyone happier. Now, there's one last thing I need to do for you, Madox," Veltik said as Madox let him go.

Veltik pulled a black marker out of his pocket and lifted Madox's hand to write on it. 'Mem-Co 9AM–6PM,' he wrote across his palm.

"See you on Monday, Madox," Veltik sneered cheerfully.

Fifteen Years Later...

A cloud of tears rolled down Madox's emotionless face. The gray tint of the room clung to the solemn skin of the two men still inside. The cold metal chair matched the chains and the empty beer bottle sitting on the floor. Madox's foot tapped against the ground as his head spiraled into dread and madness.

"And from there, you met Kris and lived the life you know," Denis finished.

Madox took a deep breath as his body shook with both fear and anger. "So... do you know who they're going to make me become next?"

Denis stared into the empty bottle as his eyes watered. "See you around, Madox," he said softly before walking out of the room.

Seconds later, two men walked back in with Veltik accompanying them. "I presume Denis caught you up on all the details of your life?"

Madox sat quietly while tears continued to roll down his face. Veltik walked behind him as the two men set down a small metal table in front of him. Madox's stomach dropped as terror sliced down his spine. One of the men placed a large silver revolver on the table.

"What is that? I thought you didn't kill people," Madox said fearfully.

"Oh, we don't—it's one of our greatest features. This is just something new we're trying out. You know, you were one of the first to have your entire identity fully erased. What an honor! So we thought—why not have you be one of our first test subjects once again?"

"What the fuck are you going to do to me?" Madox squirmed as Veltik placed an AMT on his head.

"Oh, don't worry. This will all be done in a second..."

Flick

The gray-tinted room sat empty except for Madox, strapped to the cold metal chair in the center. His foot tapped against the ground as the door squeaked open, revealing Veltik and two other men walking inside.

"I presume Denis caught you up on all the details of your life?" Veltik asked as the men placed a metal table in front of Madox.

"Fuck you," Madox replied, spitting on the ground.

"How kind of you... Well, what if I told you that you have a chance to leave? A chance to escape, and we will never mess with you or your memories ever again?" Veltik asked, slowly walking around the room.

"What are you talking about?"

"Just play a simple little game with me, and if you win, we'll let you go free."

"What game?" Madox asked hesitantly.

One of the men placed a revolver on the table, sinking Madox's stomach to the floor.

"What the fuck? I thought you didn't kill people!"

"Oh, we don't. The gun is completely empty. To play the game, all you have to do is put the barrel to your head and pull the trigger six times. Then place it back on the table and repeat that cycle two more times." Veltik stopped behind Madox, placing his hands on his shoulders. "Of course, you can choose not to play at any point—but you know what will happen then. And if you try anything funny, like aiming at me, you forfeit."

Madox's heart raced as his foot tapped wildly against the floor. His thoughts moved to Jasmine, Kris, and how much he hated Mem-Co.

"Fine. I'll do it..." he said grimly.

"Wonderful!" Veltik clapped as the men unrestrained Madox's arms.

Time seemed to slow as Madox's shaky hands reached for the gun. His heart pounded louder than the tapping of his foot. His fingers brushed the cold silver barrel, sliding to the handle.

"Oh, this is intense, isn't it? Can you feel your heart pounding? Your blood rushing with adrenaline?" Veltik whispered as Madox raised the gun to his head.

"Am I lying? Am I not? Is there really a bullet inside that you don't know about? Maybe there is. Maybe you're about to blow your brains out against this wall."

Click.

Madox pulled the trigger as his stomach crawled into his throat. His chest broke into uneven breaths as his finger hovered over the trigger.

"Oh wow! You're not dead yet! Do you have the nerve to go again? Or are you going to let us turn you into whatever puppet we want?"

Click. Click.

Fear turned to anger as Veltik's words boiled Madox's skin.

"HA! I didn't think you had it in you to go this far! Maybe you really will get out of here. But then what? What would you do after that? Go around preaching how bad Mem-Co is? Sorry to say, but you're the only person left that would ever think like that."

Click.

"Let's face it—you lost, Madox! No matter what you do, we are never going back to that old world filled with pain and suffering."

Click.

Madox's body shook so violently that holding the gun became difficult. His foot screamed for help as his heart felt as though it would explode. Tears poured from his fear and anger as the false memories of his life flashed before his eyes.

"Last bullet. Am I lying? Am I telling the truth? Do you have the nerve to pull the trigger?"

Click.

Madox inhaled a deep breath of relief as he threw the gun back on the table. His heart shot through his chest as his mind released its fear. Even his foot sat peacefully on the floor, at ease from what could have occurred.

"Hah, you really did it! Just do that two more times, and you're free to go!" Veltik said cheerfully.

"How are you so happy about this? I won, didn't I?" Madox asked as sweat dripped from his forehead.

"Not yet, you still have two more rounds. Even so, if you did manage to free yourself from here, as I previously stated, there is nothing you could do to hurt me or this company. So, would you like to move to round two?"

Madox sat quietly as he looked around the room distrustfully.

"Fine," he said, reaching for the gun.

"Oh, wait! We have to do something before you can go again," Veltik spoke devilishly.

"That's not what you said! You said I just have to do that two more times!" Madox shouted angrily.

"Oh, it's nothing. Think of it more as a precaution than anything," Veltik said, placing an AMT on Madox's head.

"You're giving me a new memory?!" Madox shouted as the men strapped his hands back to the chair.

"Not exactly," Veltik responded as all the men took a step back for a moment. "Alright, you're ready to go again!"

"What? You didn't even use it!" Madox shouted in confusion.

Veltik took the AMT off his head as the men unstrapped his arms.

"Correct, it's like I said, this is more of a precaution than anything. But you can go again whenever you are ready."

Madox looked around the room, beginning to understand how the game worked. He could easily get out of there as long as he pulled the trigger on his head six times. His fear dropped from his chest like an anvil as joy shot through his veins. Madox realized he would escape, having already won the difficult part of the game. There was nothing more to do than put the gun to his head and pull the trigger to let him walk out scotfree.

Click. Click. Click. Click. Click. Click.

Madox pulled the trigger all six times without hesitation.

"Oh, confident now, are we? Place the gun back on the table, and if you choose, you can go one more time, and we will let you go free," Veltik spoke in his same sunny tone.

Madox placed the gun back on the table, setting his arms on the metal chair. The men strapped him down once again as Veltik placed the AMT on his head. Madox could feel his insides almost bursting with confidence as he knew escape was inevitable.

"Alright! Last time!" Veltik shouted. "Are you sure you want to go again?"

"Yes, now unstrap me," Madox responded angrily, ready to leave this pointless game as Veltik took the AMT off and the men unstrapped him from the chair.

Madox reached for the gun without hesitation, placing the barrel to his head.

Click. Click. Click. Click. Click.

Bang!